Flipping

Eichin Chang-Lim

First Edition published by Dog Ear Publishing
Second Edition published by Eichin Chang-Lim
December 2016
www.eichinchanglim.com

Cover Art by Victoria M. Lim
Book Interior by The Book Khaleesi

ISBN-13: 978-1541303584
ISBN-10: 154130358X

Table of Contents

Part One

JonSun 1

    Chapter 1 3

    Chapter 2 14

    Chapter 3 29

Part Two

Elliana 53

    Chapter 4 55

    Chapter 5 77

    Chapter 6 102

Part Three

The Kids 125

    Chapter 7 127

    Chapter 8 149

    Chapter 9 180

    Chapter 10 203

Acknowledgments 223

Appendix 1 225

Appendix 2 229

About the Author 235

This book is dedicated to my good friend and colleague, Dr. Bill Takeshita.

Bill, your journey to blindness has inspired many low-vision patients and people in similar conditions as yours. I am so proud to know you.

Also, this book is for all the people who face their shortcomings and strive to reach their aspirations with courage.

Part One

JonSun

Chapter 1

A ll I want is to see her one more time and get to know her name. Am I expecting too much?

JonSun Tang scanned the library hopefully just as he had every time he'd been there in the last two months. But just as they had been each previous time, his hopes were dashed when a quick but thorough check of the stacks proved fruitless.

I'll never see her again, he despaired.

He'd done the math: the National Taiwan University campus was 1,086,167 square meters with more than 20,000 students… the chances of randomly running into each other were not good. Encountering her even *once* seemed like a miracle. He could recall every moment of the meeting in vivid detail.

That fateful September day, the air was thick with unfallen rain. The steel and concrete of the towering metropolis absorbed nothing, trapping the moisture in the congested streets, where it instantly condensed on the skin of the commuters as they hurried along their way.

JonSun breathed heavily as he chained his bike on the

rack by the entrance of the main library. Sweat trickled down his forehead. He needed to grab a book for his International Macroeconomics class term paper. It had only just been assigned, but JonSun wanted to get started on it as early as possible.

He walked under the grand arched entryway of the brick library and pushed open the heavy door. Only a few students were inside, casually glancing through books rather than poring through them with hunched shoulders, as they would be during midterms. *Probably more interested in club meetings and parties than their studies*, he thought. That was a luxury he didn't have.

Once he removed the book from the shelf, he waited absentmindedly in line — until he locked his gaze on the figure ahead of him at checkout. Her khaki skirt was short and tight enough to reveal her legs and heart-shaped butt, but long enough so that it wasn't too revealing. Her sleeveless maroon shirt revealed her toned, bare arms. She spoke in a sweet tone that hovered on the air. A butterfly-shaped clip held back her glossy black hair and reflected the overhead light.

She hadn't even turned around yet and JonSun felt like he'd been struck by lightning. He had to try a few times before he could successfully swallow.

Suddenly she made a quick turn and bumped right into him.

"So sorry," she said. She abruptly turned her head and revealed apologetic eyes and a pristine, makeup-less face.

Her front side is as attractive as her backside, he found himself thinking.

Before he could muster any words, the beautiful vision with the jasmine-scented hair and lilting voice started toward the door.

FLIPPING

A rush of adrenaline suddenly emboldened him—he could go after her and ask for her name! Just as he stepped forward, though, the lady at the desk stopped him.

"Are you ready?" she asked, her stern mouth dragging him to reality.

"Oh, yes," he stammered, handing her the book. "I want to check this out." When he looked back toward the door, the girl had disappeared.

Why didn't you talk to her when you had the chance? he asked himself once he left the library. But he knew why. She was way out of his league. Not only was she exceptionally lovely, but by her Louis Vuitton bag and impeccable Northern Taiwanese accent, it was obvious she was a day student as well. And day students didn't date night students.

Nevertheless, her image lingered in his head. He found himself searching for her on campus. He adjusted his schedule so he always went to the library at the day and time they had met in the hopes that it was a time she would be likely to return.

If you ever see her again, he told himself, *you will at least talk to her.*

He had almost abandoned hope when one day he walked into the library only to see the same sleek head with barrettes buried in a book at a long table. His pulse quickened. Without a thought, he sat beside her.

"Hello," he said, his mind racing a mile a minute. Should he be humble and deferential or strong and confident? Women didn't seem to fall for "nice" guys, but he didn't want to come off as arrogant or pushy either. He tried to plow a middle row. "Do you mind if I sit here?" He hoped she didn't notice his imperfect Mandarin with its Southern Taiwanese accent.

"Sure," she said, looking up and giving him a brief smile before returning to her book.

JonSun craned his neck to see what she was reading. "English?" he asked.

She nodded. "That's my major."

"I love English," JonSun fibbed, desperate to keep the conversation alive. Then a flash of inspiration hit him—so brilliant that he decided it must have been sent from above. "Did you know they're having an English-language film series at the local movie theater this weekend?" he asked as casually as he could manage. He'd just happened to see a flyer posted.

"Really?" she asked, seeming genuinely curious.

"Yeah, I was thinking about going..." he continued, "but I don't know anyone who'd be interested."

Before he knew what had happened, JonSun had the dream girl's name (SuAnn Chen) and the promise of a date for that Friday night! He couldn't believe his luck. It was somewhat daring for a good Taiwanese girl to agree to go out one-onone with a boy, and yet, SuAnn seemed every bit as modest and traditional as he could hope for. Wasn't this a sure sign she must really like him too?

JonSun's feet barely touched the ground on his way back to the tiny room he shared with three other night students. On the wall he noted a calendar, announcing the date as November 13th. From that day on, he decided, thirteen would be his lucky number.

✤ ✤ ✤

JonSun couldn't think about anything but the upcoming date all week. He ate rice and beef broth for both lunch and dinner each day so he would have enough money to cover the evening, and he scouted the area near the theater for an affordable place to take SuAnn after the movie—if she'd let him.

He was thrilled to learn that the movie showing Friday night was *Casablanca*, touted as one of the most romantic movies of all time. *It's like everything's falling into place; like it's meant to be.*

On the night of the date, JonSun was about to leave when his roommate, Huang, stopped him.

"Oh, no," Huang said, shaking his head. "You're not wearing *that*." Huang considered himself something of a ladies' man, and he had decided to take the inexperienced JonSun under his wing, regularly giving him unsought big-brotherly advice on how to meet and woo women. Usually JonSun ignored him since he wasn't interested in the kind of women Huang pursued, but tonight he thought he might benefit from Huang's worldliness.

JonSun looked down at his outfit. He didn't have anything except his worn-out clothes, and he'd chosen the least worn of those.

"You're too tall for my pants, but here's my lucky shirt," said Huang, tossing it to JonSun. "The ladies love it."

JonSun rubbed his hand along the silky black fabric, so much finer than the coarse material of his own. Shrugging, he pulled off his shirt, revealing a slim torso, well-muscled from a lifetime of physical labor.

Then Huang ruffled JonSun's stick-straight hair into a looser, windblown style. Stepping back to observe his handiwork, he nodded approvingly and pushed JonSun in front of the mirror.

"You'll have her eating out of your hand."

FLIPPING

JonSun rolled his eyes, but in truth he was rather pleased with the image that was reflected back. *I don't look half bad.*

✥ ✥ ✥

SuAnn met JonSun outside her dormitory building. She wore a lavender dress with a pink cardigan sweater. If it was possible, she was even more beautiful than he remembered her.

"That's a pretty dress," he said, thinking that SuAnn's shapely curves made the dress rather than the other way around.

"Thank you," she said, lowering her eyes modestly.

They got to know each other a little on the way to the theater. As they walked past the bookstores, clothing stores, and cafés surrounding the campus, JonSun learned that SuAnn was one of four daughters, and her father was a surgeon with a successful practice in Taipei.

A surgeon! JonSun couldn't help but think how he wished the boys back home could see him now: their favorite whipping boy enrolled at University in Taipei and now taking out a stunning surgeon's daughter! The look on Wu Chien's face would be priceless.

In the theater, at first JonSun was so aware of SuAnn's presence beside him that he had trouble concentrating on the film. But soon he was swept up in the moving tale of the embittered WWII nightclub owner who was reunited with his lost love only to selflessly give her up in the end. When the lights came back on, he hoped SuAnn didn't notice him surreptitiously wiping tears from his eyes.

"Would you like to stop somewhere for a drink? Uh, tea or coffee, I mean…" he stammered.

SuAnn smiled. "Yes, I'd like that."

JonSun led the way to the small café he had picked out earlier, a tiny oasis from the hustle and bustle of the busy street just outside.

"Tell me a little about yourself," SuAnn requested after they were seated.

JonSun generally avoided talking about himself, but SuAnn was so easy to talk to, before he knew it, JonSun found himself telling her all the things he usually took pains to hide. He told her how his father's farm in the southern end of Taiwan had been destroyed by the frequent typhoons that had pummeled the coast when JonSun was just a boy, leaving his father unable to support his wife and two children.

He told her about his erratic education, patchy from stints working in the fields, his father's valiant but unsuccessful attempts to find employment after the loss of the farm, and the family's struggle to get by on what his mother could bring in as a maid and his own meager earnings both before and after his father's death from pneumonia.

He didn't tell her about the near-daily taunting at school, the schoolyard fights, his father's spiral into drinking, his mother's resentment, his parents' arguments, all the nights he and his older sister, JenJen, had gone to bed hungry. But what he told her was more than he'd ever revealed to anyone.

SuAnn took it all in stride. She listened compassionately without a trace of what JonSun feared more than even her contempt: her pity.

"So now you are working full time and going to night school?" she asked. "That's a lot to take on." There was admiration in her voice.

It *was* a lot. Between supporting himself, paying for university, and sending money home to help his mother on the paltry wages he earned as a maintenance worker for the university, JonSun wasn't sure how he was going to manage it financially. But what worried him most was the schoolwork itself. His spotty education hadn't adequately prepared him for college-level classes, and he was having to work twice as hard as his peers just to catch up.

"I'll make it work," he said.

"Yes," SuAnn said, contemplating him thoughtfully. "I believe you will." The simple statement struck JonSun at his core. It wasn't just a polite throwaway comment. She said it with a calm conviction that made JonSun believe he *could* do it.

With this woman behind me, I could do anything.

But, of course, he knew that could never be. The fact that she'd agreed to a single date was already more than he had any right to hope for.

After hearing about JonSun's childhood, SuAnn began to tell him about her own. Her father was a driven, ambitious man. Despite the great success he had achieved in his medical practice, however, he was deeply dissatisfied and bitter because he had no sons to join him in the practice and carry on the family name. It didn't matter how much money or professional respect he attained; for a Taiwanese man, the inability to produce a son meant he was a failure.

As the youngest of the four daughters, SuAnn had borne the brunt of her father's displeasure. "My mother was already quite old when she had me," she said. "I was his last chance for a son, and I don't think he has ever forgiven me—or her." She shrugged. "Maybe that's why I am so interested in America," she said. "I spent my whole childhood daydreaming about running away and starting over in a new world."

FLIPPING

JonSun was surprised. "Do you still want to live in America?"

"Oh, no," she said, shaking her head dismissively. "My father wouldn't hear of it. He has big plans for me. Since I couldn't *be* a doctor, I'm supposed to *marry* one. That's why I'm here. For my MS."

JonSun's heart sank. He'd known he stood no chance with her, but this just sealed the deal. He was an economics major, not a future doctor.

Still, there was something special between them, something he'd never felt before. An ease, a comfort that had allowed him to tell her things he'd never told anyone else. They just seemed to click.

Suddenly, JonSun noticed the waiter beginning to mop the floor. It was closing time! They had been so deep in conversation that they hadn't realized the time. Apologizing to the staff for holding them up, JonSun hurried to pay.

All too soon, the night was over and they were back at SuAnn's dormitory door. A goodnight kiss didn't even cross JonSun's mind. She was *much* too much of a lady to subject to such a serious impropriety.

"Can I see you again?" he asked hesitantly, steeling himself for the inevitable rejection. Casual dating was unknown in Taiwan, and given SuAnn's father's criterion for prospective sons-in-law, JonSun wasn't a candidate for more.

"How about next Saturday?"

JonSun nodded eagerly.

"Good," she said with an impish smile. "Meet me in front of the foreign languages building at six. I've got a surprise for you!"

✤ ✤ ✤

FLIPPING

JonSun spent the week reliving every precious moment of their evening together. He couldn't believe he'd told her so much about himself, revealed the humiliating past he generally took such pains to hide. But he couldn't bring himself to regret a single word. Her warm acceptance had been like a balm on his soul.

As their next date neared, JonSun wondered what her "surprise" could be. He couldn't come up with a single guess. Her mischievous smile haunted his thoughts and danced in his dreams.

On Saturday night, JonSun was a half an hour early. He needed to calm down, he told himself sternly. There was no way the night could live up to his fantasies. *You're setting yourself up for disappointment.*

The instant he saw SuAnn, though, his worries disappeared. Not only was she more beautiful than he remembered, but the way she lit up when she saw him made him feel like he owned the world.

"Have you been waiting long?" she asked.

"Not too long." *For you.*

"Are you ready for your surprise?" There was that bewitching smile again. "Good. C'mon, follow me." She led him into the building and to a small student lounge equipped with a television and VCR. "The foreign language department has a collection of English-language movies available for students," she explained, taking a video out of her bag.

"*The African Queen?*" JonSun read in his halting English.

"It's another Bogart film," she explained. "With Katharine Hepburn."

And so began a tradition. During the week, they led separate lives. JonSun worked all day and went to class at night, while SuAnn studied and socialized with her friends. But the weekends were theirs. They quickly fell into a habit of spending their Saturday nights watching English-language movies—especially old Hollywood classics.

Before the school year ended, they had advanced to holding hands on Royal Palm Boulevard, with the first scenes of their love tenderly framed on either side by enormous palm trees and scented with wild pink azaleas. Even nature seemed to celebrate their young love.

Finally, on their very last night before SuAnn left campus for the summer break, they visited Drunken Moon Lake and walked along the bridge. The green roof of the lake's cabana stood out against the fiery orange sky, and the entire picture before them was reflected in the glassy water, as still as could be. There Jon-Sun worked up the courage to give SuAnn a chaste kiss. The pressure of their lips sent an electric current throughout Jon-Sun's body; every cell seemed to hum and vibrate.

The memory of that kiss sustained JonSun all summer.

Chapter 2

J onSun worried that things would be different in the fall, that after spending so many months at home with her family, SuAnn would have come to her senses and realized their relationship had no future.

But, the instant they saw each other, it was as if not a day had gone by. They resumed their weekend movie ritual. Having exhausted the university's supply of '30s and '40s classics, they moved on to later decades and discovered a mutual love of Neil Simon, Alfred Hitchcock, and *Butch Cassidy and the Sundance Kid*.

JonSun didn't venture another kiss—that was a glorious magnificence reserved for special occasions—but the hand holding, which by itself was practically a promise of engagement, continued.

Still, they never spoke of the future. This indirection wasn't unusual for Taiwanese couples, who relied on suggestion and innuendo, but JonSun's reticence was more than cultural reserve. He worried that if he broached the topic of marriage, the obstacles they faced would become painfully real. He preferred to linger for as long as possible in their present bubble of happiness. After all, it might be all they ever had.

FLIPPING

✤ ✤ ✤

One balmy evening as JonSun and SuAnn were coming back from watching *The Graduate*, the door to SuAnn's dorm flew open and a petite, middle-aged woman shot out as if from a cannon.

"SuAnn!" she shrieked. "SuAnn, where have you been?"

SuAnn shot JonSun a nervous glance.

The tiny tornado came to a halt right in front of them. She looked JonSun up and down. "And who is *this*?" she sniffed disapprovingly.

"This is my friend JonSun, Mama."

"Pleased to meet yo—" JonSun started.

Her mother snorted and, ignoring him completely, turned back to her daughter. "SuAnn, what were you doing with him when you *know* you were supposed to meet Chun-Lieh tonight? After all the trouble we went through to set up this meeting and you stand him up, make him lose face? What am I supposed to say to his mother?"

"I'm sorry, Mama," SuAnn said, lowering her head penitently. "I...forgot."

"Forgot? *Forgot*? After three months of planning?" She grabbed hold of SuAnn's arm and started dragging her toward the dormitory porch.

SuAnn had just enough time to give JonSun one last miserable glance before she was whisked inside.

Stunned, JonSun just stared at the closed door for a long moment. SuAnn was seeing other men? His stomach churned so violently he thought he might vomit.

In a daze, he stumbled home. Unable to sit still, he paced the miniscule room like a lion in a cage. Although he was too respectful to ever have talked about SuAnn before, JonSun was so overwhelmed that his roommate Huang was finally able to coax the story out. He shook his head sympathetically.

"That's tough, mate."

JonSun lay awake all night. Sleep was an impossibility. As soon as it was daylight, he went back to SuAnn's dorm and waited outside the door. When she finally emerged two hours later on her way to class, he pulled her toward a bench where they could talk with some degree of privacy.

"What was that about?" he demanded with no preamble.

"I'm sorry. It was my mother—"

"You were supposed to see someone else?" he interrupted.

SuAnn looked away. "He's a medical resident. My mother has been wanting to set me up with him for a while. I don't know where she finds them all…"

JonSun was stricken. "There have been *others*?"

SuAnn admitted that her mother and grandmother were actively attempting to match her with a fresh medical school graduate; she'd been introduced to a dozen guys bearing the M.D. title.

"But I only go to make them happy," she assured him, "to keep them from suspecting I'm already…involved. If they knew about you, we'd have no peace. For us to be together, I *have*
to go."

As little as he liked it, JonSun knew she was right. It was excruciatingly clear that after her failure to produce a son, SuAnn's mother was dead set on procuring an acceptable son-in-law. If she had any notion that SuAnn had serious feelings for JonSun, she would do everything in her power to keep them apart.

He wondered aloud if their cover had already been blown, but SuAnn told him that she had been able to convince her mother that he was just a friend walking her home from a late night of studying, and that the introduction to Chun-Lieh would be rescheduled for another time under the fiction that SuAnn had suffered an incapacitating twenty-four-hour stomach virus.

"All right," JonSun reluctantly agreed, "you should go. But you *must* promise me that you will tell me about any future 'introductions.' You can't keep them from me ever again."

"I promise," she said, taking his hand in hers.

They seemingly returned to life as before, but their idyllic bubble had been burst. SuAnn's family's disapproval was no longer a vague, theoretical concept; it had taken on flesh and blood dimensions. JonSun could not imagine this woman, who had looked through him as if he didn't even exist, *ever* deigning to accept him as a part of her family.

And would SuAnn, so docile and deferential, have the nerve to openly defy her family's wishes? He knew she cared about him, but what if she recognized the relationship would never be anything more than a college romance and was only trying to prolong their time together before inevitably giving in and settling down with a suitable husband? Were they living on borrowed time?

JonSun couldn't bear to know, so he didn't ask.

When the date of SuAnn's meeting with Chun-Lieh arrived, JonSun spent the day in a paroxysm of white-hot jealousy. Afterward, SuAnn assured him that Chun-Lieh had been, like all the other young doctors before him, a son of wealth and privilege, with an unbecoming sense of self-importance and entitlement.

"Medical school is hard," she said, fixing him with a meaningful look, "but there are many things far harder."

JonSun breathed a sigh of relief. He was fortunate that the stereotype of the arrogant, egotistical doctor was overwhelmingly true, but how long would it be before she would run into one of the exceptions? He dreaded every new "introduction" and spent the time waiting crippled with debilitating fear.

His roommate Huang was no help. "I like SuAnn," he said, as JonSun paced back and forth. "I do. And I believe she truly cares about you. But she's a *good* girl. When it comes down to it, she's not going to disobey her parents."

"But she's not even that close to them," JonSun insisted.

"That just makes it worse. If she's been chasing their approval all her life, she's not going to give up her best chance to get it. You've got to be prepared. I don't want you to get hurt when it happens. Just try to enjoy it while it lasts."

By the end of their second year, JonSun could feel himself distancing from SuAnn. He still loved her more than ever, but the "introductions" were sheer torture, and no matter how hard he tried, when he tried to envision a future together, he just couldn't see it. Family was central in Taiwan—the locus of almost all social activity—and he would never fit into SuAnn's.

Maybe it's better to get it over with. It'll only hurt more later.

But before he could convince himself to make the break, something happened that changed everything.

⁂ ⁂ ⁂

JonSun got a letter from his older sister, JenJen. She had fallen in love with a Taiwanese-American who was temporarily working in Kaohsiung, and they were planning on getting married and moving to America. Once there, she would sponsor their mother for immigration, and him too, if he wanted it.

America! JonSun felt a sudden jolt of hope. He couldn't see a way for him and SuAnn to be together in Taiwan, but in America?

As he mulled the idea over, JonSun found himself getting more and more excited. America might offer him better prospects than he faced at home. Taiwan's economic boom of the '80s had slowed considerably, and hiring and advancement were still largely determined by birth and connections.

America was still seen as the land of opportunity. *They don't care where you came from. All that matters is how hard you work.* He could succeed somewhere like that, couldn't he? Sure, he'd need to work on his English, which was still far from fluent, but he knew enough to get by...

Slow down, JonSun, he told himself. *It's not a done deal yet.*

Would immigration even be possible? Just because JenJen was a citizen didn't necessarily mean his immigration was assured. Would there be other requirements to meet? He'd never considered immigration before and it was a complex, opaque process.

He couldn't wait to see SuAnn to see what she would say. Sure, she had fantasized about living in America as a child, but there was a big difference between childhood dreams and adult realities. Would she really be willing to sacrifice everything she had ever known for an uncertain future in a distant land?

He hurried over to the library to wait for SuAnn to get out of class. When he saw her walking up the path, he suddenly became nervous. He realized that the entire course of his life might hinge on her response.

He intercepted her and took her by the elbow, steering her away from the library door. "Let's go for a walk," he said. "I've got something I want to talk to you about."

She looked at him curiously. "Okay."

"I just got a letter from my sister," he began. "She's marrying an American and moving to California. She'll be a citizen and she can sponsor me for immigration." He hesitated. "Would you...would you want to go to America with me?"

SuAnn stopped. Her eyes were as round as teacups. "America? Really?"

JonSun nodded.

"I always imagined what it would be like living there, but I never *really* considered moving..." She looked him right in the eye. "What do *you* think?"

"I think if you were with me, we could make it in America. Really make it."

SuAnn just stared at him, her face betraying nothing of what was going on in her mind. It was the longest minute of his life.

"Yes, I think we could," she finally said.

"You'd do it?" JonSun asked incredulously. "You'd leave your family? Your friends? Everything?"

"Could we live in Hollywood?" she said, a mischievous smile playing on her lips.

JonSun picked her up and spun her around. "We can live wherever you want!" He let her slide down his length and kissed her on the mouth long and deep.

A Hollywood kiss.

FLIPPING

‡ ‡ ‡

JonSun thought he and SuAnn couldn't get any closer, but having a real, tangible goal to work toward added an entirely new dimension to their relationship. With SuAnn's help, Jon-Sun doubled-down on his English, and they spent their free time learning all they could about their country-to-be.

Everything was imbued with a sense of excitement and infinite possibility. It was the adventure of a lifetime, and they were doing it together!

Even SuAnn's introductions didn't bother JonSun anymore. She was firmly committed to him, to their new life together. Their plan was to get married right after graduation and emigrate as soon as they had saved enough money for the plane tickets and immigration fees. At first they would live in San Francisco to be near JenJen, and when they had gotten their feet under them, they'd take off on their own.

‡ ‡ ‡

The time seemed to fly by, and before they knew it, graduation was upon them. SuAnn graduated with honors, while JonSun had ranked solidly in the middle of his class. But as the first in his family to attend college, JonSun couldn't have been prouder. He only wished his father could have seen him accept his diploma.

"A good education is the golden key to a good life," his father, who had only made it to junior high, had always said.

"This is for you, Dad," he whispered, running his fingers over his new diploma.

Since SuAnn and JonSun were in different colleges, they didn't go to each other's ceremonies. SuAnn's family attended her commencement and threw her a party afterward. Jon-Sun's mother had already left to join his sister in America, so after briefly celebrating with some classmates, he went home to an empty apartment.

SuAnn was able to steal away long enough to call JonSun from the party.

"Are you ready for tomorrow?" he asked.

Graduation was only part one of their grand plan. They would be getting married at the District Court the next morning. They had already filled out their marriage agreement and marked it with their chops, a small stamp bearing their names in ancient Chinese script. JonSun had enlisted Huang to stand up for him, and SuAnn's college friend, Liu, was to be their second witness.

"I had such a good time with MeiYin today," said SuAnn, "I'm thinking about asking her to come to the marriage ceremony, maybe even be a witness." MeiYin was SuAnn's older sister. Having graduated a couple of years earlier and still unmarried, she was the only one of the four daughters living at home.

"Are you sure she'd support it?" JonSun asked. "She doesn't even know about us yet."

"I know, but she'll be on our side," SuAnn assured him.

Jon-Sun knew from what SuAnn had told him that MeiYin was chafing under their parents' restrictive "doctors-only" dating policy. Not blessed with her sister's good looks, it was uncertain if MeiYin would get married at all.

"Maybe our marriage will even pave the way for her," said SuAnn. "Besides, it would mean a lot to have someone from my family there."

JonSun didn't think the marriage ceremony was the best time for a first introduction, but it was bad enough SuAnn would have to forego any of the rest of her family being there. This was the least he could do. "If it means that much to you..."

"Oh, thank you! I'll ask her tonight."

That evening, as JonSun was laying out the clothes he was going to wear the following day, there was a loud knock at the door. He opened it to a tall, stern-looking man with silver hair. Although he had never met the man, JonSun recognized SuAnn's father from pictures. He knew instantly what had happened. MeiYin had betrayed them.

Mr. Chen strode in, sweeping the tiny, sparsely decorated room with his icy gaze before fixing his attention on JonSun himself. His eyes bored into JonSun, who began to wilt under the unrelenting stare.

"So, you think you are going to marry my daughter?" Mr. Chen said.

"Um, yes, sir."

"Against her mother's and my wishes?"

"I love SuAnn," JonSun replied, struggling mightily to keep his voice from quaking.

"Love?" sniffed Mr. Chen scornfully. "Love is as flimsy as soap bubbles on the water. It's lovely. It's pleasant. But it can't support a marriage."

JonSun summoned every ounce of courage he possessed. "You can't stop us. We don't need your permission. We are adults—"

"Adults?" scoffed Mr. Chen. "SuAnn is a child. A romantic child. And you are taking advantage of her innocence to steal her away from her family to take her to...what? What can you offer her?"

JonSun's mind went blank. What *could* he offer her except

himself? He had nothing but his hopes and dreams and willingness to work.

"Exactly," SuAnn's father said when JonSun didn't reply. "You're a *farm boy* from a nothing village. And now you've got yourself a degree from *night school*—not even honors."

Feeling the heat rising to his face, JonSun was suddenly ashamed of the degree he'd worked so hard for, and humiliated for having been so proud of it.

"What do you think you're going to get with *that*?" Mr. Chen continued. "You've got no contacts, no connections. What, do you think they'll just be handing out jobs when you get off the plane in America? I'll tell you what's going to happen. You'll take SuAnn away from everything she's ever known, only to have her live in some rat trap like this" —he looked around disparagingly— "surrounded by strangers, when she could be here, in the bosom of her family, leading the kind of life she's accustomed to, the kind of life *I* can afford to give her. Did you know that SuAnn has never cooked a meal on her own? Never had to iron a shirt or scrub a toilet? She has *no idea* what she's signing up for. She's never known anything but a life of plenty and privilege. But you have."

He suddenly became conciliatory. "*You* know what it is like to live on the edge. To be poor and hungry and desperate. To pray you don't get sick because you can't afford to go to the doctor if you do. To work your fingers to the bone and still not know if you'll have enough money for rent. Is that what you want for SuAnn?"

JonSun couldn't speak.

Mr. Chen continued, almost fatherly now. "I believe you are a good man, JonSun. A man of integrity. I need you to do the thinking for both of you. If you *really* love SuAnn as you

say, you will do what is best for her, even when she doesn't know what that is. I trust you will step
up and do the right thing."

He seemed to take JonSun's silence as acquiescence. He extended his hand, which JonSun accepted mechanically.

With that, Mr. Chen left as abruptly as he had come.

JonSun looked down at the envelope in his hand. Inside were ten crisp five-hundred-Taiwanese-dollar bills.

JonSun lay awake, going over and over what SuAnn's father had said. He felt certain the man didn't give a damn about what was good for SuAnn. All he cared about was fulfilling his plan to secure a doctor son-in-law and sparing himself the humiliation of having a daughter who "married down." That would be an intolerable blow to his overblown ego.

And, yet...his self-serving agenda didn't automatically mean he was wrong.

SuAnn *had* been sheltered, pampered even. What did she know of difficulty? Was she really prepared for the life they were about to embark upon? What would that life even look like? Was her father right...was he headed for failure? Would he be unable to adequately provide for SuAnn and their children? Had he been a fool to think his fortunes would be any different in America than they had been in Taiwan?

The jeers that had followed him throughout his childhood rose again in his memory. *Dumb egg! Rice container!* JonSun put the pillow over his head, trying to drive out the mocking voices.

His attempts to catch some sleep failed. The dreadful scenes, buried in the deepest part of his memory, started surging up…

Being skinny and short, he had been the target of bullying in the playground.

It was a bright winter day in the southern part of the island. He saw himself, a ten-year-old, underdeveloped boy desperately wanting to be included in the games, standing on the sidelines, waiting patiently. The soccer ball finally flew in his direction, and he gave it a mighty kick. It was a powerful one!

However, the force taken to do that also tore his old, two-sizes-too-small, thin pants right at the seam between the buttocks. His faded, graying-blue underwear revealed. Girls behind him laughed out loud. A group of kids rushed in before he could hide away. The giant boy, Wu Chien, pushed him facedown, some boys pinned him on the ground, and others reached in to open the rip wide apart. The bell rang; all the kids ran away. JonSun slowly rose up, his thighs and lower legs exposed. He walked into the classroom a few minutes late.

"JonSun, come up here to the front. You are late," his teacher said coldly. JonSun walked sleepily. "Pick up your things and go home."

JonSun sensed the suppressed giggles around him. He heard the open, mocking laughter echo through the room and hallway as he walked out of the classroom.

Ha-ha-ha! Ha-ha-ha!

He opened his eyes. The streetlight cast its light inside. The lizard on the ceiling stared at him.

Are you laughing at my misery as well?

With a sinking feeling, he considered the possibility that letting SuAnn go *was* the right thing to do. If he went to America alone, she could marry someone able to provide her the lifestyle she was used to, the lifestyle she deserved.

But then something inside him rebelled. He *loved* SuAnn! And she loved him. Didn't that mean something? And who was to say he couldn't be successful? It wasn't a sure thing, but whatever advantages of birth he lacked, he made up for in drive and determination. If he was given a fighting chance, he was sure he could give SuAnn a comfortable life, a life that would make all her sacrifices worth it.

Or was he just being selfish?

✤ ✤ ✤

In the morning, JonSun still hadn't made a decision. Every time he thought he had made up his mind, he would immediately begin to second-guess himself, launching into another exhausting round of deliberation.

Huang, who had been out celebrating all night, stumbled in bleary-eyed and reeking of liquor.

"Lemme just grab a shower," he said, "and I'll be ready to help you bolt on the ball and chain."

"I'm not going through with it," JonSun said dully.

"*What!?!* You've been wanting this since the day you met her, and you're backing out *now*? It's just cold feet, mate. I know I tease you about getting tied down, but you're a one-woman man if I ever saw one. What's gotten into you?"

JonSun told him about Mr. Chen's visit. "As much as I don't want to admit it, I think he might be right."

Huang was at a loss. "She's a smart woman," he said. "She knows what she's doing."

"Maybe," JonSun said, shrugging noncommittally.

Huang took his shower and, running late, they hurried to the courthouse. Whatever happened, JonSun knew he wasn't about to leave SuAnn at the altar, wondering why he never showed up. He'd at least do her the courtesy of breaking up with her face-to-face.

Chapter 3

The appointment with the judge for the civil wedding was at 11 a.m. The day before, SuAnn had insisted on meeting a half an hour earlier.

"So, we have some time to settle in before the ceremony," she said.

JonSun and Huang arrived at the courthouse right at 10:30. The magistrate's office was on the second floor. They flew up the stairs. JonSun looked around for SuAnn, but she wasn't there. *That's unlike SuAnn. She's never late.*

The minutes ticked by. Still no SuAnn. To calm himself down, JonSun signaled Huang to sit down on the bench in front of the office and wait. Huang hung his head down and dozed off almost immediately. JonSun surveyed the surroundings, attempting to distract his raging mind. The air was damp and mixed with the mild lemon-pine scent from he floor cleaning agent. Some dust had accumulated at the edge of the wall. *The maintenance guy had obviously not done his best job.*

A young man passed by, crumpled a piece of paper into a ball, and fiercely aimed at the trash can in the corner. The paper ball hit the rim, jumped out, bounced off the wall, rolled a few feet, and rested there lifelessly.

FLIPPING

It was 10:45. Still no SuAnn.

JonSun stood up and walked downstairs.

I'll stand by the entrance; she will be able to see me right away once she gets here.

Minutes later, there was still no SuAnn. The security guard shot him a suspicious look. JonSun lingered a little longer, averted his gaze to avoid the guard's scrutinizing stare.

His heart sank deeper and deeper. The air became suffocating. His undershirt was soaked with sweat and clung to his skin.

He walked back up to the second floor.

A couple had just emerged from the magistrate's office. She was dressed in a long white gown and held a bouquet; he was in a tux. It appeared to be a completely traditional wedding ceremony.

It's supposed to be our turn now. Where's SuAnn?

JonSun began to wonder if perhaps she wasn't coming. Had she changed her mind on her own? Or had her father changed it for her? Was it possible he was even physically preventing her from coming, hoping that delaying it would derail the wedding altogether?

He was convinced that SuAnn would not show up. He tapped Huang to wake him from his deep sleep.

"What happened?" Huang muttered.

"Let's go. She stood me up." JonSun was saddened.

Then—suddenly—SuAnn was running up the steps and down the hall toward him. She looked radiant in a simple ivory sheath dress.

"I'm so sorry!" she exclaimed breathlessly. "My father...he tried to stop me from coming." Her friend Liu appeared at the foot of the steps.

FLIPPING

Seeing SuAnn again, all JonSun's good intentions flew out the window. He simply couldn't bring himself to break things off. He took both her hands in his and looked straight in her eyes.

"SuAnn, are you *sure* this is what you want to do? I don't want to come between you and your family. I don't know what fate has in store for us, what kind of a life I'll be able to offer you…"

She squeezed his hands. "I'd rather take my chances with you than live a life of luxury with anyone else. We're in this together—sink or swim!"

JonSun crushed her to him, then pulled her, laughing, toward the magistrate's office, Huang and Liu following behind.

As they repeated the traditional marriage vows, JonSun made his own vows.

I'll make sure you never regret the faith you put in me today. I won't let you down. I'll give you the life you deserve if I have to move heaven and Earth to do it.

After the wedding, instead of the lavish wedding banquet with seven hundred guests and twelve dishes at a five-star restaurant that her sisters had had, JonSun and SuAnn visited the Shilin night market. There they sampled several of the Taiwanese snacks being hawked by vendors: deepfried chicken breasts, oyster omelets, stinky tofu, and panfried tapioca cakes, all washed down with a cup of pearl milk tea.

Although there were many stalls selling their wares, the couple preferred the carnival games to shopping. JonSun tested his mettle at pinball, Mahjong Bingo, and the shooting gallery, all in an effort to win a prize for his new bride.

"I'm going to get that rabbit if it takes all night," JonSun exclaimed after he shot only six of the ten balloons in one of the games, netting him a paltry number of stamps.

"You could just buy a rabbit. They sell them on the other side," SuAnn said, laughing.

JonSun pretended to be scandalized. "A rabbit cannot be *bought*. It must be earned. With cunning and prowess and lightning-quick reflexes." He demonstrated his best martial arts moves with mock seriousness. "You must be shown what an extraordinary warrior your new husband is."

JonSun handed over the money for another game, and this time managed to score an even less impressive five balloons.

"Is it too late to get out of this marriage?" SuAnn asked.

JonSun shrugged. "Possibly. There is a certain...technicality that I plan to resolve in *very* short order." He drew her close and whispered in her ear. "And then there'll be no escape. You'll be mine forever." His voice was husky with desire.

With difficulty, he pulled himself away and continued his quest for the elusive stuffed rabbit, teasing and joking as before. But all he could think about was what was to come later that night. All the waiting and wanting of the last four years was over.

He couldn't believe that he would finally be able to express his love in what was simultaneously the most primal and sacred of acts. Not just once, but for the rest of his life. She would be his.

His wife.

✤ ✤ ✤

FLIPPING

The next day, the newlyweds awoke languorously to the morning sun streaming through the window, at last husband and wife in every sense. In their first official act as a married couple, they sent back the money SuAnn's father had given JonSun.

They took a small flat near the university to save a nest egg for their move. JonSun kept his old job while hunting for a college graduate position. SuAnn busied herself learning to cook and keep house for the first time. JonSun was amazed by the creativity she demonstrated in decorating using only what they had or she could find for free; he was always coming home to an artful arrangement of handpicked wildflowers or a piece of furniture reclaimed from the dump and given a second life. Their entertainment budget was also zero, but they didn't mind. Who needed to go *out* for entertainment when they had each other's bodies to explore in exquisite detail every night?

The first few months of married life flew by—tarnished only by SuAnn's estrangement from her family. Before they knew it, six months later they were at the San Francisco International airport, hearts in throats, waiting to meet JonSun's mother, sister, and brother-in-law.

"Welcome to America!" JenJen shouted when she spied him from behind the gate.

Soon they were all hugging and shaking hands and talking over one another. SuAnn and JonSun's mother hit it off right away, and JenJen's new husband, Lee, seemed like a nice enough fellow, if a little on the geeky side.

✣ ✣ ✣

FLIPPING

At first, they stayed on JenJen's couch while JonSun tried to find a job. Since they didn't know where his job would take them, they decided SuAnn would wait to look for a job until he found his. However, she helped him craft his résumé and look for openings. Of the hundreds he sent out, he received a handful of interviews, but he never got an offer, or even a call back. JonSun became increasingly discouraged.

What was it? Was he doing something wrong, making some terrible gaffe that marked him as a dumb farm boy who had no business being there? Or maybe his language skills were holding him back. In four years he'd made significant progress in English, but he still wasn't fluent; he knew his accent was heavy—sometimes impenetrable—and he often didn't have the vocabulary to express what he was trying to say.

As the weeks dragged on and their nest egg dwindled, Jon-Sun passed from discouraged to desperate. What made it worse was the nagging voice telling him that SuAnn's father had been right. *You're worthless. Nothing. You'll never make it. And now you've brought SuAnn down with you, you selfish jerk.*

Finally, at the end of his rope, JonSun saw an ad for a property maintenance position at a condominium complex in Los Angeles and applied for it.

"It's a glorified handyman position," JenJen told him. "You don't even need a degree."

It was also half as much money as the corporate jobs he'd been applying for. But it was a job.

Since he had no car, JonSun had to ask his sister to make the 400-mile trip to Southern California for him to interview for the position.

"Of course," she readily agreed. "If that's what you really want."

FLIPPING

JonSun was offered—and accepted—the job on the spot. He didn't mind the nature of the work—in fact, truth be told, he'd always enjoyed his handyman job more than his schoolwork—but he felt like he was letting his father and SuAnn and himself down by not using his degree. Nevertheless, he and SuAnn packed up their belongings and set off for Los Angeles County.

"We're going to Hollywood!" SuAnn chirped happily, never so much as hinting that the job was several steps down from what he had been aiming for.

They checked into a hostel and SuAnn quickly found a position as a bank teller at an Asian bank, earning quite a bit more than JonSun, which he tried not to let bother him. JonSun knew it wasn't anything she was passionate about, and he hoped she wouldn't have to work there long, but when they started looking for an apartment to rent, he was shocked at much of their earnings would go toward housing costs alone.

After passing on several apartments, their Realtor, Jim, convinced them to look at a third-floor walk-up that was outside of their budget.

"It may be more than you were hoping to spend, but considering what it has to offer, it's actually a bargain," he promised.

As soon as they walked in, JonSun could tell SuAnn was taken with the huge windows and historic details. She deserved it. *And so much more.* They signed the lease.

"I can't wait to decorate," said SuAnn. "Maybe someday I'll take some interior design classes."

FLIPPING

Her outlook on the future seemed rosy, but JonSun felt that his dreams were falling farther and farther out of reach with every day that went by. The longer he went without a corporate position, the less chance he would ever get one. The property maintenance job, while he liked it, had no possibility of career advancement, and even with SuAnn working, they were barely able to put away any money at the end of the month.

He'd wanted to be such a big success that he'd prove his father-in-law and the kids from school how wrong they'd been about him, but now he'd whittled his dreams down to owning a home and eventually putting his kids through college. And even those seemed like they might be unattainable goals.

You're a failure. A nothing. Dumb egg! Rice container! The nagging voice echoing in his head consumed him.

❖ ❖ ❖

One night after a delicious meal of lemon chicken and pineapple fried rice, SuAnn confronted him.

"You aren't happy," she said. "What's the matter?"

"I feel trapped," he said. "We're barely making it; we're not saving anything. If we keep going along this way, we'll never get ahead. I don't want to look back in ten years and be in exactly the same place we are right now. You working, living paycheck to paycheck, trying to raise kids in some tiny rental…"

"What do you want to do?"

"I don't know," he said miserably. "I already tried everything I could to get a better job."

"Okay," she said slowly, "if we can't earn more money, maybe we can make what we have go further."

"What do you mean?"

"Back in Taipei, we were getting by on one salary *and* saving money. We can be a lot more frugal than we're being."

JonSun instantly resisted the suggestion. He wanted to give her *more*, not less.

"We're not doing anything extravagant," he said sullenly.

She shrugged. "I know. But we could do *so* much better if we made that our priority. C'mon, it can actually be sort of fun if you feel like you're working *toward* something. I bet if we *really* tried, we could have enough for a down payment for a house in a couple of years!"

JonSun's ears pricked up. A house was the jewel in the crown of his ambitions. If he could own his own home, he might not have the kind of success he'd dreamed of, but he wouldn't be a failure.

They sat down and started to brainstorm all the ways they could save money. *This* was something JonSun knew all about. If saving money was a field of study, he'd have had an honorary doctorate.

They sold the two used cars they'd just bought and started taking public transportation. They stopped eating out and going to movies, except for a half-price matinee once a month. They became regular library patrons and scoured the city for free events. They froze all spending on clothing, clipped coupons for groceries, and virtually cut meat out of their diet.

But most importantly, they broke their lease on the cute walk-up apartment and moved in to the one-room maintenance office at the condominium complex JonSun managed. He convinced the owners to let them live there for free since it would allow him to be on the premises around the clock. He installed a shower in the bathroom and a tiny kitchenette in one corner.

On his better days, JonSun could agree with SuAnn— sometimes it was like a game trying to scrimp and save—but other times he would look at SuAnn trying to cook a meal on their hotplate in the shabby room and he would be consumed with shame.

This is exactly what I didn't want for you...and exactly what your father predicted.

✢ ✢ ✢

By buying virtually nothing except food and health insurance through SuAnn's job, they were able to put away nearly 80 percent of their combined income, and just a year and a half later, they had saved enough for a down payment on a beginner house.

"Time to start house shopping!" JonSun said as they celebrated the achievement by splurging on oysters and yellow wine. He decided to call Jim, the Realtor who had shown them the first apartment.

"I don't know," said SuAnn, reminding him how Jim had talked them into a more expensive place than they'd intended. "He's quite the salesman." She didn't mean it as a compliment.

JonSun shrugged. He liked Jim. Although it was true he was as loud and flamboyant as JonSun was quiet and reserved, something about him reminded JonSun of Huang.

"He didn't force us into taking it—that was our choice," he reminded her. "He was just doing his job."

"I suppose," she said, but her tone was still dubious.

FLIPPING

JonSun called Jim and explained what they were looking for.

"If you're willing to put in some sweat equity," he said, "there's a property that just came onto the market that I think you should take a look at—a trust sale."

"What does that mean?" JonSun asked.

"Well, the old man passed away, and the beneficiaries of the trust, well, his three kids and ex-wife, want to sell the house and take the money ASAP. It's a great bargain."

Jim met them at the house, which was situated at the end of a cul-de-sac in a quiet neighborhood. A pair of monarch butterflies fluttered around a bed of lilacs and stands of Mexican sunflowers in the front yard. But weeds and dry spots littered the lawn, and JonSun predicted the sprinklers were broken. Regardless, he, Jim, and SuAnn opened the chipped front door.

As unkempt as the front yard was, the inside was worse. A bookshelf heaved against one side of living room wall, half broken, and would certainly fall if a small earthquake hit. The paintings were old, the carpet a soiled mound of gnarled threads and animal hairs. The kitchen appliances were rusty. The entire house smelled foul.

"Still, it's a four-bedroom, two-bath with a spacious backyard," Jim said, completely unfazed. "It's a forty-year-old house, and you just can't find a house with this big of a backyard in new construction. The original owner lived here 'til his final days. His family wanted to sell as is—that is, quickly."

JonSun did some quick mental math. Between the down payment and everything that would need to be put into the house, he thought they could afford it if they did most of the work themselves. Assuming there were no unexpected structural issues. JonSun was a respectable amateur plumber and electrician, but he was no engineer. He'd need an expert to evaluate that.

"I'm afraid you'd have to take it without a home inspection," Jim said. "It's 'as is' or nothing."

"But why wouldn't they want us to get an inspection?" SuAnn wanted to know. "Doesn't that probably mean there's something they don't want us to know?"

"Not necessarily," said Jim easily. "They may just be erring on the side of caution. If they let you get a home inspection and an issue comes up, they'll be obligated to disclose it to any future buyers. There's no upside for them."

The idea of not getting a home inspection went against Jon-Sun's cautious nature. They couldn't afford to lose everything they had worked for all this time. JonSun hired an inspector to inspect the house after all. JonSun followed the guy through the entire process. Not only did he want to make sure the basic construction was sound; he used it as a learning experience.

So, they bought the house for $189,000 with an FHA adjustable loan. They moved in and immediately began the renovation. Every night when they got home from their jobs, they would roll up their sleeves and set to work.

Although JonSun had plenty of construction experience back in Taiwan, he had to learn how to make sure everything was up to code. SuAnn, meanwhile, worked with the design professionals at Home Depot to give their house a sleek, modern, *American* look.

They started with the bathrooms. They scraped out the current floor and the outdated pineapple wallpaper, knocked out the flimsy bathroom tile, re-grouted the tub, and repainted the walls. Soon the drab gray and blue of the bathroom was replaced by Italian-looking tile, black and gold accented walls, and a sense that they could actually become clean in their own shower.

"Hey, Su, how much have we spent at Home Depot these days?" JonSun joked. "We should have bought the Home Depot stock."

Next, they moved on to the kitchen. They repainted the cabinets, replaced the plastic-like countertops with granite, and selected hardwood floors with a pristine dark finish. Room by room, they completely renovated the entire house. It was their child, and they were proud of it. More than anything, the two loved the experience they gained by working shoulder-to-shoulder toward a common goal.

Just as the renovation neared completion, they got wonderful news: SuAnn was pregnant!

JonSun was ecstatic. For the first time since he graduated from college, he felt like a genuine success. He had provided his wife with a beautiful house that they owned, and now they were going to start a family! What more could he ask?

They decided to throw a small party to celebrate, and JonSun invited Jim to attend. "He'd probably like to see what we did to the place," he told SuAnn.

"Ah, I see, you want a chance to show off," she teased.

"Absolutely not!" JonSun protested, pretending to be grievously offended. But the truth was he was proud of his work and eager to show it to someone who knew how far it had come.

When Jim toured the house the night of the party, he was even more enthusiastic than JonSun could have hoped for.

"You did this all yourself?" he said admiringly. "You did a fantastic job! Everything is professional caliber. I could sell this place for 400K easy."

JonSun's eyes nearly popped out of his head. *"Really? That much?"*

"Sure. It's a seller's market. Prices just keep going up and up and up. Why? Do you want to sell?"

JonSun hadn't even considered the idea, but the possibility of an enormous profit certainly made him think about it.

That evening after the guests left, he talked it over with SuAnn. It was not easy to put the revamped home on the market. After all, it was their baby. They had poured their collective energy into it for two years.

"Do you really think we could get that much?" SuAnn asked.

"I don't know," JonSun said with a shrug. "That's what he said."

"It doesn't hurt to try," SuAnn said. "Let's put it on the market and see what happens."

❖ ❖ ❖

Jim held an open house for the following weekend. The prospects were amazed at the beauty of the interior design and landscaping. The backyard was luxurious not only due to its size, but the verdant gardens, a newly erected wall, and beautiful paving stone pathways. They oohed and aahed over the bright, modern kitchen and the handsome hardwood floors in the living room. JonSun grew a little taller with each compliment.

They got six offers right after the open house. The house was in escrow in two weeks and sold at $435,000. With that, they turned around and started looking for another house. Again, Jim found them an underpriced property at a desirable neighborhood being sold "as is."

"It's a divorce sale. The sellers wanted to sell it fast!" They beat out other buyers with a "cash" buy.

The purchase price was almost identical as the first one, but it didn't need quite as much work.

"You guys made out like bandits," Jim said on the way out of the closing. "Have you ever considered doing this professionally?"

"What?"

"Flipping houses. It's a lucrative business, and you've got the skills for it."

"I don't know…"

"The reason I'm asking is I just found a real steal of a deal for a condominium complex near Redondo Beach. It's poorly managed, half of the units are vacant, look shabby, and it's going for two point five million, but I think you could get it for two point two. With some work—just some cosmetic stuff—it could be worth three point five or four. That neighborhood is on the upswing. Especially as it's walking distance to the beach."

"But I don't have that much money. That's out of my league."

"Don't worry about that. My family owns an international trading business, so I've got access to plenty of capital. I'm always running into these great deals, but I don' t have any way to capitalize on them. I don't have the experience or interest in fixing them up myself. That would be your role. I'd find the properties and put up most of the capital, you'd manage the renovations, then I'd sell them and we'd split the profits fifty-fifty."

"That's quite an offer," JonSun said cautiously. "You barely even know me."

Jim shrugged. "I go with my gut. Always have. And my gut tells me you're a responsible, hardworking man who is just looking for a chance to get ahead. How does it sound, being your own boss and taking control of your financial destiny?"

What it sounded like was JonSun's dream come true.

"Uh, I'll have to talk it over with SuAnn," he said. "But I'm definitely interested."

"Of course, of course," Jim said, slapping him heartily on the back. "You do that."

❖ ❖ ❖

When JonSun told SuAnn about the offer that evening, she had questions.

"I know you like him, but do you really want to be business partners with him? What if he makes all his decisions this way—no research, just flying by the seat of his pants?"

"Maybe that's why we'd make a good team. Balance each other out."

JonSun was surprised at how much he wanted this, *needed* it even. The flame of his ambition had died down, but the pilot light had never gone out, and now it had exploded into a raging fire.

"Think about what this could mean, SuAnn! I'll never make any more than I'm making now in this job. This has *unlimited* earning potential. You could quit the bank and stay home with the baby. And help out with the interior design. Wouldn't you like that? It's a chance to *really* make it."

A chance to prove them all wrong.

Seeing how keen JonSun was to end his days as a wage slave and test his mettle in the big leagues, SuAnn easily agreed to let him take his shot.

"A bet on you is one I'm more than willing to take!" she said.

In short order Jim had his lawyer draw up the paperwork, JonSun put in his notice, and they began negotiations on the condominium complex. SuAnn decided to keep her job at the bank until things were more settled.

The day of closing, Jim showed up with an attractive but heavily made-up woman on his arm. She was at least ten years Jim's junior. Her clingy red dress was a bit too much for JonSun's tastes, as was the plunging neckline. She wore diamond earring studs of at least one carat on each earlobe with a matching necklace and bracelet. Her long red nails reminded JonSun of dragon's talons.

"JonSun," boomed Jim, "I'd like you to meet my wife, Gigi!"

"Pleased to meet you," JonSun said, extending his hand to her. "I didn't realize you were married," he said to Jim.

"Just took the plunge!" Jim chuckled. "We've only known each other a couple of months, but it just felt right. Didn't it, honey bunny? So I decided, what the heck, why not just pop the question?" He gazed at his new bride adoringly.

I guess it isn't just business decisions he makes impulsively, JonSun thought with a wry grin.

Although Jim and Gigi seemed to be playing footsies under the table, the closing went smoothly, and immediately afterward JonSun got started on the renovations. He preferred to do all the work himself, but to speed things up, he occasionally hired recent Chinese immigrants to help out. He enjoyed being able to give people good, honest work, and they were certainly worth it.

SuAnn's pregnancy also proceeded easily. She passed all

her checkups with flying colors. However, she opted not to get an ultrasound or find out the baby's gender.

"I'd rather not know," she said. "I want it to be a surprise."

❖ ❖ ❖

Seven months later, both JonSun's "projects" were nearing completion, and Jim was constantly teasing him about which one would be delivered first.

"SuAnn, you're going to have to hop to it, if you want to beat JonSun. He's just got some finishing touches to go," Jim joked when he had them over to his house for dinner one night.

Their house was situated at Rancho Palos Verdes, a gated community with a magnificent ocean view. Gigi had ordered in a virtual Chinese banquet, far more than the four of them could eat.

After dinner, they retired to the living room. Jim left to get some cigars and SuAnn excused herself to use the restroom — in her last trimester, it seemed that she was in the bathroom more than she was out of it.

Gigi moved in and sat on the couch next to JonSun, tilting her head with a curled smile.

"Jim said you're going to make him a fortune in flipping houses. That's awesome," she purred.

Before JonSun knew what was happening, her right hand crawled up his thigh and beyond — boldly exploring territory she had no business even touching. In his haste, he jumped up and knocked into the legs of the coffee table. The force upset the decorative tray of oranges. One of the oranges rolled down onto the carpet. JonSun and Gigi both attempted to pick it up simultaneously—and cracked their heads.

Jim walked in just as they were straightening up. "These are real Cubans," he said, offering one to JonSun.

"You know, SuAnn is very sensitive to smell right now," Jon-Sun said, grabbing SuAnn's hand as she emerged from the bathroom. "It's been nice, but maybe we should call it a night."

Wow, that was close! he thought as he hurried SuAnn out the door.

He tried to put the incident behind him, but the next day, he got a call from Gigi. "I'd like to discuss some business with you. Would you meet me at Tony's restaurant at Redondo Beach Pier for lunch?"

"I, uh, can't make it," JonSun said. "Sorry, I've got to go now." He hung up without even waiting for her to respond.

What should he do? Should he tell SuAnn? Should he tell Jim? JonSun had an aversion to inserting himself in other people's personal business. Did he want to be responsible for causing problems in their marriage—possibly even ending it? Would Jim *want* to know? But on the other hand, was it fair to Jim *not* to tell him?

What if he told him and Jim didn't believe him? Would this end their business partnership? The Americans had a colorful saying about shooting the messenger. Then again, even if he didn't say anything, that didn't mean the whole thing would just go away. Once Gigi realized he wasn't going to respond to her advances, he wouldn't put it past her to try to turn things around by saying *he* had come on to her.

He wasn't safe no matter what he did.

Jim stopped by the work site later that day.

"Jim," JonSun said, "there's something I need to talk to you about."

"Sure, what is it?"

"It's, uh, about last night…" JonSun said haltingly, feeling like each word was another nail in the coffin in which his dreams were buried. "I, uh, don't want to cause any problems, but after dinner Gigi, she, uh, touched me, uh, in a way only a wife should."

Jim's face hardened. "Gigi's a real touchy-feely kind of girl. Are you sure you didn't just misinterpret her friendliness for something more? We're a lot more open here about those kinds of things than they are in your culture."

JonSun wanted to be able to agree, to brush it off as a simple miscommunication. But there was no ambiguity. He'd understood all too well what she'd had in mind.

"I don't think so," he said. "She called me today wanting to have lunch. Did she mention anything to you about that?"

"Okay. Thanks for letting me know." Jim's tone was clipped. "I'm going to head off now."

"Sure," said JonSun, just as eager for the painful discussion to be over.

�֍ ✤ ✤

JonSun didn't see Jim for the next three days. He didn't drop by the property as he usually did to check on their progress and shoot the breeze.

Unable to stand it any longer, JonSun called him under the pretext of asking a question about the paint colors in one of the units. The call went straight to voice mail, and was never returned.

FLIPPING

With every passing day, JonSun grew more and more sure that he'd made a terrible mistake. He still hadn't told SuAnn, not wanting her to worry. She had enough on her mind with the baby coming any day now.

Finally, the next Monday, Jim stopped by the property. He was haggard and unshaven.

"Are you all right?" JonSun asked.

"I want to dissolve our partnership," Jim said. "I've already had the paperwork drawn up."

JonSun's stomach dropped. *Idiot! Fool! Dumb egg!*

"Jim, I'm sorry I got involved. I should have minded my own business. But do we have to let it end everything? Can't we work it out?"

Jim smiled grimly. "You don't understand. I'm not mad at you. I'm glad you told me. It couldn't have been easy. At first I didn't want to believe it, but I hired a PI and he found out she's carrying on with not one but two other men!"

"I don't understand. If you're not mad, why do you want to end our partnership?"

"I'm divorcing Gigi. Thank goodness my lawyers forced me to get a prenup, so she can't get to anything I brought into the marriage. But we bought this place after we got married, so she's entitled to fifty percent of any profits I make from the sale. And I'll be damned if that woman gets a dime from me! I want you to buy me out now, before we sell."

"But you know I can't afford that."

"I wouldn't be so sure," Jim said. "You bought your house cash, right?"

JonSun nodded.

"You can take out a fifty-thousand-dollar home equity loan. I've talked to my lawyer and banker, and my attorney

49

has already given the agreement a green light. The papers have been drawn." He pushed them under JonSun's nose.

"I can't agree to this," JonSun objected, quickly scanning the contract. "You'd be taking a big loss."

"I *want* to take a loss," Jim assured him. "If we make a profit, half of it will go to her, and I'd rather cut out my own tongue than give her a *dime*. Do you understand? Think of it this way: who deserves my money more, the loyal friend who stuck his neck out for me or the lying, cheating bitch who screwed me over? Please, do this for me," Jim pressed when JonSun didn't reply. "I'm asking you as a friend."

Before he could answer, JonSun's phone rang. SuAnn's number flashed across the screen. She almost never called him at work.

"It's time!" she cried. "I'm on my way to the hospital now. Meet me there as soon as you can!"

"Uh, huh. Of course." JonSun hung up. Jim grinned knowingly at the stunned look on his face.

"Baby on the way?"

JonSun nodded.

"Congratulations, old man!" Jim said with genuine delight. "Consider this a gift for the baby. You can sign the papers while I drive you to the hospital."

JonSun stumbled after him, his mind reeling. He was going to become a business owner and a father, all in one day? He could barely comprehend it all.

✣ ✣ ✣

I did it. I made it!

There was only one thing that could make it any better.

FLIPPING

Of course, he told himself, he'd be happy as long as SuAnn and the baby were healthy. But deep down, he couldn't deny the fact he was hoping for the ultimate blessing, to achieve the one thing every Taiwanese man wanted and his father-in-law hadn't been able to pull off.

Oh, please. Please let it be. Let me have a boy.

Part Two

Elliana

Chapter 4

I t's not a boy!" Mitch McMeri shouted excitedly. Then, he repeated it a second time, just a couple of notches below screaming volume. "It's *not* a boy!"

After nineteen hours of labor pain, Mitch and Elliana McMeri's baby was delivered by cesarean section. Elliana's lower body was blissfully numbed by the epidural; her half-closed eyes demonstrated she was finally pain-free and relaxed.

"We need to suck out the extra mucus in baby's lung," the nurse said, talking her patient through the final steps, and checking the newborn scoring.

Dr. Winn added in some reassurance too. "Everything is going well—you may feel a bit of a tug and pressure now…" He proceeded to suture the little incision that served as the tiny infant's entrance to this world.

In the midst of the flurry of actions and excitement, Elliana slurred nonsensically, "Okay! Don't tell me it's a monkey if it's not a boy."

Earlier that year, when Elliana had been twenty weeks into her pregnancy, she went in for her scheduled ultrasonic scan. The ultrasound technician and doctor both mentioned a shadow between the tiny legs.

"It's very possibly a boy," the doctor said.

Elliana nodded. It was her first child, so she had no expectation except that it would be a healthy baby. Mitch's family, on the other hand, had very *definite* preferences.

"*Another* grandson?" Mitch's mother Rose had asked. Her lower lip pouted dejectedly. After a moment she shook her head, causing her multicolored, dangling earrings to jangle. "I have three sons and four grandsons already! When will I get a granddaughter?"

"She was never one for tact," Mitch muttered to his wife.

Elliana wanted a girl eventually and understood her mother-in-law's dream of dressing a little girl as a little princess—a rapidly diminishing prospect.

But during the delivery, even during Elliana's contractions, the nurse told her that the baby's heartbeat was around 130.

"A lower heart rate below 140 beats per minute means you're having a boy."

"Yes, we know. We're naming him Christopher."

And now, after all that, they'd had a girl!

Both Elliana and Mitch were elated, as if they were astronomers who had just discovered a new planet. Since Elliana was sedated, Mitch reacted for the both of them.

"We didn't prepare for a girl," Mitch said slowly. In spite of his shock, he couldn't take his eyes off the tiny face in the pure white blanket.

Elliana thought about the name Christopher. *It's easy enough to switch to a girl's name,* she thought.

"How about naming her Christa?" she suggested.

"Christa," he said, trying the name out on his tongue. "Yes. I like it."

By the time, Elliana and the baby were transferred to the recovery room, the new parents were accustomed to this change in events. Even in the beginning, their daughter was full of surprises. Somehow, they knew that she would be anything but predictable.

✧ ✧ ✧

It was a quiet moment at around 1 p.m. in the afternoon on a sunny April day in Torrance, a peaceful suburb in Southern California. The birds were singing and tender leaves were eagerly sprouting after winter. Mitch was beside himself with jubilation.

"What a great day for my daughter to be born," he said, glancing out the window at a world that now seemed faultless to the new parents.

He leaned over Elliana, who was holding her new bundle of joy. She looked up with a face still dewy from the trying and lengthy labor. Having pulled her hair back in a ponytail, her rosy face leaned in to the one she and Mitch had created. This little girl was exactly what everyone hoped for.

"I know your mother will be especially happy," she said.

Mitch rushed to the pay phone at the corner of the hallway. He extracted a couple of coins from his pocket and dropped one in his haste to call his mother. Quickly bending down, he scooped them up and stood up, pounding his mother's number into the phone.

"Hello?"

"Mom, it's a girl!" Mitch said without introduction. He could not contain his excitement.

FLIPPING

"What did you say?" His mother gasped. "A girl?"

Then Mitch heard a loud banging noise. He would soon learn that his mother was so overjoyed by the news that the phone accidentally flew from her hand.

✛ ✛ ✛

Elliana had never felt so tired in her life. It was an exhaustion that settled in her very bones. But none of that mattered. Her joy was like a supernova. Every time she looked at the little prune-like face, the chubby legs, the delicate, tapered fingers with their miniature nails, she was struck anew by how miraculous it all was. *This perfect little being came from us?* Elliana asked herself incredulously. She had had many months to think it over, and it was still just as amazing now — if not more so.

Little Christa began to moan. Clumsily, Elliana shifted the child in her arms and gently tilted her head toward her to nurse. The act was so very intimate. It was the basic but incredible act of giving life. Nothing would give her more fulfillment than those precious moments with her daughter.

As Christa sucked lustily, Elliana's gaze fell upon the calendar on the fridge. *Just one more week.* She stood up abruptly, accidentally dislodging the baby, whose forehead wrinkled in consternation. Elliana recognized the look and rushed to guide Christa back to the nipple before the storm broke. Then she carried her out of the room, away from the accusing stare of the calendar.

That evening, when Mitch got home, he found Elliana in the nursery, staring into the crib. She looked up at him.

"Honey, I just don't think I can do it," she said.

"What do you mean? I think you're doing great."

"No, it's not that. I just don't think I can go back," she said.

Mitch sighed. Elliana's job as a regional representative at a pharmaceutical company in Irving, California, visiting numerous practitioners throughout Los Angeles and Orange County to promote the new drugs, was demanding even without a child.

"I don't know what to do," Elliana whispered as she and Mitch stared down into Christa's crib. She smoothed out a tiny wisp of golden-brown hair swooped across the crest of their baby's head. "I'd only be giving each job fifty percent of my attention, and motherhood takes a hundred percent."

Mitch bit his lip. "We'll have to take a look at finances."

A music teacher and band director at the local junior high school, Mitch loved his job and couldn't imagine doing anything else. But it didn't pay very well.

Elliana laid her hand on top of Mitch's and squeezed it reassuringly. "I know. It's not going to be easy. We'll have to really buckle down and discuss this."

Mitch nodded. "But I know it's important. Trust me. My mom stayed at home too, and even though we didn't have a lot of money in those days, having her raise my brothers and me was more than worth it. I wouldn't mind working extra hours if it brought more money…oh, wait! Private lessons."

Elliana's ears perked up at that proposition. "I like the sound of that! Didn't you used to do that for middle school kids back when you were in college?"

"For a while, yeah. I don't know why I stopped, really."

"If we cut back on our spending, we might not need you to pick up much extra work," Elliana said, leading him away from their sleeping cherub. "I'll get out a spreadsheet and we'll nail down some numbers."

FLIPPING

She moved the tall, thin flower vase with a half-bloomed rose stem from the center of the dining table to the counter. In no time, she was surrounded by randomly scrawled notes of ideas for extra cash, a spreadsheet of finances, and their taxes from the previous year.

"It's not going to be easy," he said, tapping his right temple with his index finger. "I just want us both to realize that."

"I know," Elliana replied. "But it's very doable."

"As long as you understand, I'm okay with giving it a go."

When a babbling Christa awoke from her nap an hour after their logistics meeting, their hearts melted. They knew they were making the right decision. Without further ado, Elliana put in her two-weeks' notice at her job in Irving.

✤ ✤ ✤

Ellie used the brief respite of Christa's nap time to put in yet another load of laundry. *No one told me how much laundry I'd be doing with a newborn,* she thought. *And here I am using cloth diapers!*

After the challenges and rewards of a high-powered career, she was surprised at how much she enjoyed the simple pleasures of caring for her daughter, cleaning the house, and spending a therapeutic hour or two cooking for dinner.

The phone rang, and Ellie rushed to answer it before it rang a second time. She didn't want to risk waking the baby, even though Christa was turning out to be a remarkably sound sleeper.

"Hello?" Elliana balanced the phone on her shoulder while he stuffed another load of baby clothes in the washer.

FLIPPING

"Ellie." The voice was hushed, urgent. "Is that you?"

The voice on the other end of the phone took Elliana back in time.

"Oh." Elliana dropped what she was doing and devoted her attention to the phone. "Is this... MayLan?"

"Yes. I wanted to stop by in an hour. Are you busy?"

"Uh, wow." Truthfully, it wasn't the best time to have company—she turned and looked at her hopelessly cluttered home. She was going to pick up a little after the laundry. But MayLan's tone was distressed. "Well, as long as you don't mind the state of my house, then I'd love to have you."

"Good. I'll see you soon." MayLan hung up as suddenly as she called, leaving a befuddled Elliana on the other end.

She frowned.

Ever since they got married, Mitch and Elliana had hosted international exchange students. Elliana had studied abroad in Spain when she was in college, and her host mother in Spain had made her feel like family. Elliana wanted to give that same experience to the students they hosted. Their most recent student had been a sweet girl from Taiwan named MayLan, who stayed with them for a school year.

And now she was dropping by out of the blue.

To prepare for MayLan's imminent visit, Elliana made a mad dash to the living room and threw different toys, freshly dried clothes, and odds and ends in closets and random nooks and crannies of the house. She told herself she'd return and clean more thoroughly later.

After brewing a new pot of hazelnut coffee, she heard the expected loud knock at the door.

"Hi MayLan," she said, smiling bashfully. Elliana belatedly realized she had stained jeans on and a plaid button-up with all the buttons in the wrong holes. Her hair was back in a ponytail, so thankfully her visitor wouldn't see the rat's nest she hadn't combed out earlier.

"Hi," MayLan said. She was unsmiling and had a touch of another emotion on her face that Elliana couldn't quite put her finger on.

Very odd, she thought. Certainly, MayLan was there for counsel...

"Well, come in! It's been so long since I've seen you. I'd hug you but I don't know if you'd want to get that close to me right now." She laughed nervously.

MayLan clasped her hands together and walked in. Her gaze was distant.

"Let's go in the living room," Elliana said. "Luckily Christa's asleep, so I won't be too distracted."

"Ah," MayLan said, turning her attention to Elliana more fully now. "I forget! How is your daughter? And...having a daughter?"

"It's hard," Elliana admitted. "But it's the best hard work I've ever had. I could drop a few clichés about how it's the most fulfilling role ever, but I won't bore you."

MayLan frowned; Elliana realized she might not have known the word "cliché."

They sat in the living room, with Elliana on the green recliner. After exchanging a few more pleasantries, Elliana cut to the chase, which is what she figured MayLan truly wanted to do.

"So...what brings you here today?" she asked.

MayLan swallowed. "If it not too much, I need to talk. About some things."

Elliana noticed her English had improved since she saw her last time. She enunciated "some things" instead of "some tin." A touch of worry entered Elliana's heart now. MayLan was clearly struggling with emotions that she couldn't verbalize in her broken English. *I hope it isn't anything serious,* she thought.

"Well, the reason of my visitation. It is that I did something... something b-bad." MayLan broke off and tried to regain her composure.

Elliana leaned in and told her that she could say anything she needed to. It emboldened MayLan to go on.

"I drink one night. I met this man. White man. He drink too..."

MayLan recounted her tale quietly, unable to look Elianna in the face. She had gotten drunk at a party on Valentine's Day with a group of international students. MayLan could barely recall the evening; however, when she woke up the next morning beside a guy she hardly knew and saw the evidence of their torrid activities, she could guess what had happened.

Fast-forward a couple of months. MayLan was now pregnant. Her shame was weighing her down, and she had no idea what to do.

"I beg you for help," she said, tears threatening to overflow onto her cheeks. "I cannot go home. This would bring much dishonor on my family. I..." She finally let the tears flow. She buried her face in her hands, and her shiny black hair fell over them and covered her flushed face.

As shocked as Elliana was, she was relieved it wasn't a death. If she were in a different place in life, Christa's birth would have caused plenty of issues too. She couldn't imagine the complications of culture, especially since it wasn't just out of wedlock, but the result of her only one-night stand in another country!

"Shh, it's okay," said Elliana, wrapping her arms around her young friend. "Don't worry right now. We just need to discuss this logically. Let's think about our options."

MayLan pulled away. "Options?" she asked, aghast. "I cannot go home with baby. Just...no. I can't." She broke into a new onslaught of tears. "I cannot do that to my family."

Elliana felt helpless. The alarm it caused MayLan struck her heart. She had never known such fear.

"What about adoption?" Elliana gently suggested. "It might be difficult for you, but you would bring another family *such* happiness."

"Adopt?" Elliana saw the gears in MayLan's mind ticking as she considered it. "What about you? Oh, Elliana, you would take it?"

Elliana pulled back. "I don't know about that. Why don't we look into an adoption agency, though?"

MayLan nodded, but she also wouldn't drop the idea. "But I know you. It would be such easy process. I would know my baby go to a good family." Her words were serious. They had been thought through and rehearsed carefully.

Elianna realized her visit was not a random act; it had a specific purpose. She was still too shocked from the news to respond to her pleas.

"All I can tell you, MayLan, is that I will be here for you. We will get through this together."

✛ ✛ ✛

After MayLan left, Elliana pinched the bridge of her nose and tried to clear her head. She slumped into a chair and listened to the clock tick by.

FLIPPING

Questions exploded in her head like popcorn kernels in a popper. They couldn't do this, could they? It was crazy to even consider it. They'd just had a baby themselves and were wondering how to make ends meet with just one child, much less two!

Christa's insistent wail cut though Elliana's jumbled thoughts. Her daughter was staring out of the crib with curious blue eyes when Elliana walked in.

"Hey, little girl," she said, gently picking Christa up. She settled herself in the rocking chair, latched Christa on, and rocked back and forth as she nursed her child. The feeling was warm and comforting. Christa looked up at her mother with wide eyes that slowly became weighted; her blinking slowed down until her eyes closed.

Elliana stroked her baby's silky pink hand, singing the words to her favorite songs, and thought about how much she loved her daughter. There was absolutely nothing she wouldn't do for that little life in her arms. It was so powerful it was almost scary.

I would know my baby go to a good family.

MayLan's words reverberated through Elliana's mind. It wasn't about the words themselves as much as the implications of MayLan's total belief in her. MayLan trusted her as a motherly figure in her own life, and that warmed Elliana's heart. She knew then and there she wouldn't let her old friend down. But as for the adoption…

She looked down at Christa and sighed. There was no job she ever had that amounted to the satisfaction of motherhood, nothing nearly as important. *From the first hit,* she thought, *I've been addicted…*

The garage door roared open. Mitch was home. Elliana gently sat up and lay Christa in bed so she could greet her husband. He was shaking off his jacket when she entered the living room.

"Hey, honey, how was your day?"

Elliana walked over and kissed him before saying, "MayLan came over today."

"Oh yeah? How's she?"

"Not good," Elliana said. "Why don't you sit down and I'll tell you all about it."

They did just that. When he heard about MayLan's pregnancy, he was shocked, noting that MayLan didn't seem like the type to get drunk, let alone sleep around.

"And I get a feel for these things as a teacher," he added.

"I know," agreed Elliana. "I felt the same way. The way she told the story, I'm wondering if it's possible she was drugged, especially considering how she doesn't remember anything."

When Elliana got to the part about MayLan asking them to adopt the child, though, Mitch's jaw really hit the floor.

"Whoa, whoa," he said. "That isn't happening. Not with our current financial situation. No way, Elliana!"

Elliana raised an eyebrow. "What situation? We're set; we just can't be wasteful."

"Yeah... are you saying you want to do it?" He looked alarmed, hoping she was not serious.

Elliana shrugged. "I honestly don't know. Motherhood is so new...but I feel like I finally found my calling." Mitch didn't respond. She added, "Anyway, we don't need to make a decision right now. Let's just think it over."

"I know you want to help MayLan," Mitch said, "but we need to be sure this is the right thing for us, too."

Don't make decisions out of impulse, Elliana reminded herself.

She walked toward the kitchen to check on her dish of the day, baked parmesan chicken. The fragrance of the Italian seasoning permeated the room. She opened the oven door and peeked. *Ten more minutes.*

Mitch stood up from the couch and followed her. His emotion swelled. He gently turned her around and held her tight in his arms. A bear hug.

"This would mostly fall on your shoulders, and I don't want you working too hard. You do have a tendency to take on too much, y'know."

"And you've got to save me from myself?" she teased.

"Something like that. Just promise me you'll think about what it will really mean."

"Fair enough."

Over the next few days, Elliana let the idea of adoption settle in. Every time she picked up Christa, fed her, changed her diapers, she imagined doing it, not just for one, but for two. *Wouldn't taking care of two babies at almost the same age be easier than having a second child while Christa was an active toddler?*

And there was another reason to consider the adoption. Elliana had a heart condition which made pregnancy risky. She'd been willing to put her own health in jeopardy in order to start a family, but now that she had Christa, she had another life to think about. She and Mitch wanted more kids, but Elliana couldn't bear the idea of leaving Christa motherless. MayLan's situation would work out perfectly…if she could convince Mitch. She resurrected the conversation about a month later.

"MayLan is still bent on us taking her child," she said,

sliding beside him on the couch. "Of course, I recognize that might change... maybe she'll grow accustomed to the idea and want to keep it."

Mitch leaned back and stared at the ceiling. "Are you sure you want to consider this? There are so many issues. Is it even legal? Shouldn't MayLan's parents be told? It doesn't feel right keeping it a secret from them."

"I know. I feel the same way. But she'll be twenty-one when the baby's born. It's up to her whether or not to tell them. I wondered if I shouldn't try to get *her* to tell them. Maybe they wouldn't be as horrified as she is afraid of and it would all work out fine. But then again, MayLan knows them better than we do, Mitch. She's a smart girl. And it's a different culture. The stigma around unwed mothers is a lot stronger there than it is here. I really do think it could ruin MayLan's life, and the baby's too."

"Okay, fine. But even if adoption is the answer, would it be better for the child to be adopted into an Asian family where it doesn't stand out as different?"

Elliana shrugged. "But MayLan knows us. Think of the peace of mind it would give her. And I think as long as we love the child and give it a strong sense of belonging, the color of its skin won't matter."

Mitch sighed and gave her a wry smile. "Okay, back to the legal question. I assume you've already checked into that?"

She grinned back, sensing the softening of his tone. "Well, I have to admit the situation is an unusual one; friends don't often give babies away to other friends. I think that's because it can be difficult for both parties if they see each other on a regular basis. But MayLan's living so far away takes that out of the equation. I don't see any reason it can't work. MayLan isn't a minor, and even though it would be an international adoption, it looks doable."

"I'm still worried about finances. Isn't adoption extremely expensive? We were having trouble figuring out how to make ends meet already!"

Elliana slipped her hand in his and squeezed. "We just have to make it for a few years, until they're both in preschool and I can go back to work again, at least part time. In some ways, it may be easier this way. If we waited another two or three years to have our second child, it would be that many more years I'd be out of the workforce. And as for the adoption itself, I thought I could sell my silver set to cover the expense."

"But you inherited that from your mother!" Mitch said.

"I think Mom would have been tickled pink that her silver set allowed us to add to our family. It's just a thing. This is a *life*."

Mitch gave her a long look. "You really want this, don't you?"

"I just want us to have a plan… If it happens." She put her head on his shoulder.

"What if she changes her mind? I don't want you to be disappointed."

"I know that's a possibility. But honestly, I'd be okay with that. I know how strong the mothering instinct is, and if MayLan wanted to keep her baby, yeah, it might hurt, but I'd support her in any way I could."

Mitch and Elliana talked for a couple of hours and reviewed their budget again. The more they discussed it, the more real and possible it became. But it was MayLan herself who convinced Mitch in the end. She came over and made her case personally. Hearing how sure she was that adoption was her only choice, how much it would mean to her knowing her baby was in a loving family, Elliana could see from Mitch's face that he'd been won over.

MayLan continued to visit as her pregnancy progressed.

"You barely show still," Elliana said, opening the door and allowing her entry. MayLan was in her second trimester, but no one would have known. "I can't even tell you're pregnant."

MayLan gave the smallest of smiles to her host mother. "But my pants do not fit anymore," she replied.

"I bought some new tea earlier—would you like some?" Elliana asked.

"Yes please."

Elliana felt encouraged by the simple agreement. The act of drinking tea together was always warm and comforting, and she hoped it would help encourage MayLan to speak. She walked to her kitchen feeling chipper and energetically filled a pot of water.

Meanwhile, MayLan glided around the room like a specter, soundless and distant. She settled herself on the forest-green couch and stared out the window, as if to avoid contact with any of Christa's baby paraphernalia. Suddenly her eyes widened.

"What was that face?" asked Elliana.

MayLan sighed. "I felt it kick."

That comment rendered Elliana speechless. She remembered the first time she felt Christa kick. That had been the moment the baby was no longer an abstract idea, but a very tangible life form growing inside her. It was a piece of her that would grow and make an impact on the world one day. The feeling was very real, but not unpleasant... not in her situation. Elliana couldn't fathom that MayLan wouldn't have the baby. Maybe after the kick she'd keep it... *And wouldn't that make her happier?*

Later, when Elliana brought Christa down, seeing the cooing baby only seemed to make MayLan more uncomfortable.

"Would you like to hold her?" Elliana offered hopefully, trying to break the ice. "As practice?"

MayLan bit her lip. "I don't know. There are complications..." she trailed off. She was torn, wanting to hold a baby. Finally, she got tough. "Elliana, I just cannot. My family... my future..." She broke off and shook her head. "I just cannot."

"Hey," Elliana whispered, leaning over and stroking May-Lan's slender arm. "I know this isn't easy. There is no clearcut answer, and I know you're not willfully giving the baby up. But... but I talked to Mitch. About the possibility of keeping it."

MayLan's eyes widened. "Yes?"

"Yes. I think we could do it. But we don't want to make any guarantees until you know for a fact what you're getting into. I want you to have the flexibility to think about your options until the very end. Don't let Mitch and I keep you from keeping the child, if that's what you want."

MayLan's English had improved dramatically; she even awed Elliana with some advanced vocabulary. But Elliana had to remind herself to slow her speech down to ensure that May-Lan understood every single word she said. She didn't want to chance MayLan's misunderstanding her message.

"You always say the perfect things," said MayLan. Tears glittered along the rims of her eyes, but they never flowed out. "I could never have asked for a better friend."

Elliana leaned over and gave her a hug. "You would do

the same for me. I know it." As convinced as she was, it didn't keep her from feeling nervous about the responsibility. She tried to shake such thoughts away.

✢ ✢ ✢

Whenever MayLan wasn't over, Mitch was at work, and Christa was asleep, Elianna looked online to compile all the information she needed for adoption resources. They would need a résumé and they had to meet a list of qualifications proving that their home was suitable for children. Other qualifications included income tax returns, documents proving they had clean bills of health, background checks, fingerprints, and more.

Mitch rubbed his temples after reading the long list, but that wasn't all: they also recommended working through an agency and having an adoption attorney to manage the financial side.

"Are you sure MayLan is going to go through with it?" Mitch bluntly asked, leaning forward in the computer chair and staring at Elliana. "I don't want to do all this for nothing."

"Better over-prepared than under-prepared," Elliana said. "And I haven't seen her waver. Not even once."

And through the months, MayLan stuck to her decision. She seemed to want to distance herself from Christa and the baby, and Elliana didn't press her. She figured it was a defense mechanism MayLan needed to get through it.

"If only the heart and brain linked together," the young girl once remarked sadly, as close as she ever came to revealing her true feelings.

✢ ✢ ✢

FLIPPING

As Halloween decorations began popping up in stores, May-Lan continued to swell—and not just her belly, but her ankles and feet too. At once she was filled with dread and longing, as she explained to Elliana and Mitch. She wanted the baby out of her, but she was afraid of facing her decision. The McMeris shared mixed feelings as well, but tried to be excited to help lift MayLan's spirits. They had no idea if they would have a boy or girl because not knowing made it easier for MayLan to stay as distanced as possible.

It was late October, and Elliana had placed a plastic jack-o-lantern outside and strung fake cobwebs through the front porch's shrubs. She sat at the kitchen table to continue sewing Christa's Halloween costume—a ruffled candy corn dress—when the phone rang.

"Hello?"

"Ellie, it's me," said MayLan. She sounded breathless. "It's time."

Elliana shot out of her seat. "Do you need help? Are you at the hospital? I can drive you!"

"Yes, I need a ride! I'm at home."

Elliana swiftly grabbed her child, strapped her in her infant carrier in the car, called Mitch to meet her at Little Company of Mary Hospital, and drove away. She was still wearing her patched jeans and her hair was in a messy ponytail, but she completely forgot about it. Suddenly driving was a race to beat the stoplights. It was rush hour, and it seemed like they hit every red light on Hawthorne Boulevard.

Jeez, this is more stressful than giving birth! she thought. At least all she had to think about was breathing and keeping the baby from coming. Driving, especially with a cranky infant, was no picnic.

FLIPPING

When she arrived at MayLan's apartment, she ran in and tucked her arm under the young girl. "Lean on me," she said.

MayLan was still so small in spite of how large her belly was by comparison.

When they arrived at the hospital, Mitch was standing there as anxious as they were. He took over the fussy Christa immediately and kept his attention focused on the child to calm himself as much as her.

Elliana was in the delivery room right by MayLan's side, coaching her on the breathing just like they had practiced in birthing class. The baby was born only four hours after her first contraction.

"And it's a girl!" cried the nurse joyously. The baby shrieked loud enough to fill the whole room.

MayLan breathed heavily and leaned against the pillow as they took the baby away to clean her. She closed her eyes. Elliana brushed MayLan's hair back and squeezed her shoulder consolingly.

"Have you thought about a name?"

"You should name her," MayLan said. She opened her eyes and gazed at Elliana with the utmost trust.

Elliana frowned. She and Mitch hadn't even discussed a name, assuming MayLan would want that honor. She was in deep thought while the doctors cleaned up the baby, and it wasn't until she saw MayLan's jade bracelet that she had a thought.

"Maybe Jade," she said. The name had a beautiful connotation and would remind her of MayLan's favorite jewelry. That particular bracelet was from MayLan's grandmother—a family heirloom. Elliana said the name again, trying it out on her tongue. She wanted to think of MayLan whenever she saw the child, but the name needed another syllable to even it out. The name "Lynn" was a tradition for girls in Mitch's family. "What about Jadelynn?"

"Your choice," MayLan replied. "But I like it."

When the nurse brought the baby back and tried to give it to MayLan, the girl said, "It is not mine." She turned her head away as the nurse placed the still-crying babe in Elliana's arms.

Many emotions swept over the two women that day. Even though the child wasn't biologically her own, Elliana was enchanted by the little girl. She knew immediately that she would be stunning. Even though it was still flushed from her birth, her skin was like parchment and she had striking hazel eyes. And Mitch felt the same way.

"Jadelynn," he said, smiling. "A beautiful name for a beautiful girl."

As the McMeris got ready to take the baby home from the hospital, MayLan was even more distant and unemotional than ever. They decided that Elliana would drive MayLan and Jadelynn back in her car, while Mitch took Christa in his. The ride was silent except for Jadelynn's baby noises. Although she wanted to be supportive, Elliana felt that what MayLan needed most was some alone time. It was a strange position to be in—taking a child from her friend. What was the protocol on that?

When Elliana pulled up to MayLan's apartment building, she noticed tears running down the girl's face. Her heart sank.

"Hey, what's wrong?" Elliana asked softly.

MayLan shook her head. "No reason to talk about it."

Elliana paused. Part of her didn't want to press. She already considered Jadelynn her daughter. The mere thought of giving her up caused her stomach to clench into a knot of dread.

But, looking at MayLan, Elliana knew what she had to do. It was only right.

"MayLan," she said, "you know, we don't have to go through with this. Seriously, this is the last time I can offer, but I want you to know I mean it genuinely."

MayLan looked like she was falling apart, but her words were firm. "No. She's yours. Her life will be beautiful." That was the last thing MayLan said before she slipped out the door.

Elliana's heart was heavy for MayLan, but she converted that ache into energy to parent this new precious life. *I'm going to live up to her expectations,* Elliana thought that night while she watched Mitch holding Jadelynn up to her sister's crib. *Jadelynn will have a wonderful life.*

Elliana didn't hear from MayLan over the next few days. She continually wondered whether she should reach out or let MayLan have her space. After a week, she finally gave her a call only to find the number disconnected. When she went over to the apartment to investigate, she learned that May-Lan had returned to Taiwan.

"I knew she was going to go back home as soon as she could," Elliana told Mitch. "But I never thought she'd leave without saying good-bye."

Chapter 5

L ife was hectic. Having a newborn infant and a six-month old daughter was challenging, as if they had twins. Elliana was grateful that Christa was such an easy baby. She rarely cried and even Jadelynn's wails didn't seem to affect her. In fact, she slept through them all night long, with her chubby head tilted to the side and her serene face reflecting nothing but bliss.

She's already the big sister, Elliana thought. She couldn't wait to show the girls off at Thanksgiving, when the whole family would be together for the first time since Jadelynn's birth.

The McMeris were gathering with Mitch's two brothers and their families at their parents' house. Mitch's four nephews ranged from age five to ten years old, and all of them ricocheted around the house like the balls in a pinball machine. When one smacked into an adult, they took off again in the blink of an eye.

The Macy's Thanksgiving Day Parade was hosted by Katie, Willard, and Al bundled up in fashionable pea coats, wool scarves, and thick mittens. "And here comes Barney!" Al shouted.

"Look!" Elliana cried to the boys. "Barney's on that float!"

FLIPPING

The younger kids shot over to the living room and shrieked excitedly for their favorite purple dinosaur. They were captivated by the screen for a few moments, but it was fleeting. They were all energized by one another's presence and continued their frenetic romp around the house.

The older two boys were playing their newfound addiction, the Nintendo dance pad. On a particularly challenging course, they got into heated arguments.

"You're not doing it right!"

"Lose a couple pounds and maybe you could go a little quicker!"

"Boys!" their mother called, poking her head out from the kitchen. "No fat jokes."

The culprit scowled and whispered to his brother. "A stegosaurus could do better."

"Just give me another go." The losing cousin snatched the controller and was going to show him that he was only warming up.

Mitch's mom, Rose, wasn't at all interested in intervening. She couldn't tear herself away from the girls, holding Jadelynn on her hip while tickling Christa to hear her joyful shrieks of laughter.

"See how sweet the little girls are? Not like the boys!" She grinned a toothy smile and stroked Jadelynn's wisps of dark brown hair.

The wives were busy preparing dinner and chatting. The turkey was basted, the potatoes peeled, and green beans shucked. The dough for the pie was made, and one of Mitch's brothers' wives rolled it into long, thin cords before braiding it together over the top of the piquant red cherry pie. Each woman was part of the Thanksgiving meal machine and did their part to help it come out right at the end.

FLIPPING

Around noon, Elliana took turns nursing each of the girls while the men watched the Dallas Cowboys play the Washington Redskins in the adjoining room.

"That's bull!" she heard Mitch yell. The other guys grunted in agreement and shouted in unison.

They're probably louder than the children, she thought, rolling her eyes playfully. As if contesting that evaluation, Jadelynn's face contorted and she let out an ear-splitting cry. She was overtired and all the commotion did nothing to help the situation.

Elliana nervously glanced at Christa. She was lying down peacefully in the crib; her eyes slowly being weighed down by the desire to sleep. She was milk-drunk, warm, and napping in seconds.

But Jadelynn refused to be solaced. Elliana rocked her frantically, but she only grew more and more agitated.

"You are so lucky to have such a calm baby!" her sister-in-law said, coming over to stand over Christa's crib. "None of my kids would have slept through that. The slightest noise would set Tommy off."

"Mmm-hmm," Elliana said absently. But her eyes flitted to her firstborn. She had always been grateful for Christa's ability to sleep anytime, anywhere, but suddenly there was a nagging voice inside her head growing louder and louder, right along with Jadelynn's cries.

There was no way any baby could sleep through that. Something was wrong.

As Jadelynn became more hysterical, so did her mother. Elliana was frightened to even acknowledge the possibility in her mind. She wanted—needed—to convince herself it was just her imagination.

Mitch waved off Elliana's fears as they drove home. He

didn't even look at her and stared straight ahead as he steered. "I'm sure it's nothing. You're letting your imagination get the best of you. Trust me, this is a blessing. Why question it?"

Elliana turned her head and stared outside. Some houses had Christmas lights out already. She resolutely promised herself one thing: she would take Christa to her pediatrician as soon as possible. Mitch wouldn't need to know about it.

❖ ❖ ❖

Elliana dropped Jadelynn off at her neighbor Joanna's house.

"It shouldn't be long," she said apologetically, passing over the diaper bag. "In any case this coincides with her nap, so she should be quiet."

"No problem," the neighbor said. Joanna assumed it was just a routine wellness check-up for Christa, and Elliana didn't correct her.

"Thanks a lot," Elliana said. When she slowly turned around to get in the car, she bumped into the life-sized snowman at Joanna's porch by the door. "Sorry," she absentmindedly apologized.

On the way to the doctor's office, she was completely absorbed in her thoughts. Her imagination ventured to the possibilities, but she mentally slapped herself out of it. "Focus on the road, Elliana," she muttered to herself.

She opened the car door, feeling like she was moving through maple syrup. After removing her daughter from the car, she gently set her down in her stroller. She walked away a few yards before realizing she left her purse in the car. *I'm lucky I didn't forget Jadelynn,* she thought ruefully.

When her pediatrician, Dr. Zimmer, finally entered the

office, Elliana had pent up so much emotional steam that she immediately burst. "I think my daughter may be deaf!" she shouted. There, she'd said the d-word—and it shocked her even as it flew off her tongue.

Ever the unfazed professional, the doctor didn't flinch. "Let's take a look at Christa's file here and see what we see," he said simply. He avoided any assurances or false promises. Elliana was thankful for that and clasped her hands.

After he shuffled some papers around, the doctor looked up and said, "There's some good news. Christa *did* pass the infant hearing screening at the hospital, if you remember."

Even though his face was alight with optimism, Elliana paused, then frowned. It simply did not comfort her. "Aren't there any tests we could perform here?"

"Yes, we're getting to that," the pediatrician said. He still seemed unconcerned, but instead of calming Elliana, his nonchalance made her want to scream. She didn't want to be right; she just wanted to know for sure she was wrong so she could lay her fears aside.

The hearing tests were simple: the doctor extracted some rattles and shook them around Christa—who turned her little head toward the noise. *Or was it the movement?* Elliana wondered nervously. She *seemed* every bit the curious infant, enraptured by all the sights and sounds around her. Even when Dr. Zimmer stopped shaking the rattle, Christa's large eyes held onto the source of the noise she may or may not have heard.

"Really, with the screening and our diagnostics today, I truly don't believe there's anything to worry about," Dr. Zimmer finally announced.

"Are you sure?" she whispered.

Dr. Zimmer dismissed her worries, speaking meaningless

chatter that Elliana could scarcely listen to. He stuck his pen in his front pocket and closed the folder. Elliana's heart fell; she knew she had lost him. He was already mentally sailing to his next patient.

⚜ ⚜ ⚜

Elliana felt like she was the only human being with sense alive. No one understood her concerns. Not even Mitch.

"If the doctor said she's fine, she's fine!" Mitch said. His eyes were glued to the game and he was recumbent on his worn green recliner. The blue light from the TV flitted across his body in erratic shapes and patterns.

Elliana was a woman possessed. She marched over to the television and punched the power button. The game rapidly shrunk into a tiny square before it blipped out of existence. Looking like a lioness, she turned to her husband and commanded his attention.

"This is not a side conversation. This is our daughter."

Mitch looked at once alarmed and frustrated. He folded the recliner back in and sat up. "What do you want me to say?" he asked. "My honest opinion is that the doctor knows best."

"I just don't know why Christa never wakes up when Jadelynn cries," Elliana exclaimed. "It defies explanation."

Mitch rubbed his temples. "You're saying that you don't understand how our daughter is such a heavy sleeper. Some people are like that. My cousin slept through anything—my brothers and I used to steal our mom's lipstick and draw on his face while he napped. We'd have loud conversations and blast music. Maybe it's genetic." He smiled expectantly and clearly hoped that he had managed to lighten the mood. "I slept through the big earthquake when I was in third grade. It was a subject of laughter for a while."

Elliana didn't smile, but Mitch's information gave her pause.

"Yeah," she said slowly. "Maybe."

"And," Mitch said, rising from his chair, "I know how tired you are. You haven't been sleeping at all these last few nights. Things are always worse when you're tired. Remember that time we had to spend the night in the train station and the next day you were so paranoid that someone was going steal our backpacks?"

That's when she cracked a grin. It was too true.

Mitch stood closer to his wife and swept aside her hair, kissing her on the neck. "I'll take the night shift tonight."

"You said the magic words." Elliana wrapped her arms around her husband and rested her head on his shoulder. She was convinced she could fall asleep right there on Mitch's broad shoulder as her warm pillow.

❖ ❖ ❖

With Christa's first birthday approaching, Elliana's anxiety began to ratchet up again. Jadelynn was much younger but seemed developmentally advanced. As Elliana took notes at the coffee table with her babies on either side of her, she realized she was too distracted to decide on streamer and balloon colors.

Jadelynn was babbling and fussing—enjoying the sound of her own voice. Christa just sat and stared at her pink toes. She was too quiet compared to her sister. Jadelynn's advancements highlighted Christa's deficiency—whatever it was.

FLIPPING

How I wish I could tell my inner voice to shut up and believe everyone else is right. She prayed Christa would show signs of hearing. Her worries consumed her like a blazing fire. *I don't want to be right. I just want the truth.*

Elliana felt worry gnawing at her heart for weeks. Finally, she felt the strength to act upon it. She swiftly stood up, walked to the phone, and dialed Dr. Zimmer's office. Her jaw was set as each ring reverberated through her ears. "Hi, I need to schedule an appointment."

When she hung up, she didn't feel a thing. She felt no worry; there was no wringing of hands. Her emotions were turned off because she was now a robot with a mission: the truth. She would ceaselessly move toward achieving it, and nothing would stop her.

❖ ❖ ❖

The visit was spent in tearful begging. Finally, Dr. Zimmer agreed to refer Christa to a pediatric neurologist for an auditory brainstem response (ABR) test. A week after the ABR test, Mitch accompanied Elliana to audiologist Dr. Jennings' office for the result.

Neither of them spoke on the way there. Elliana sat in the examination room with her arms wrapped protectively around Christa, prepared for the worst.

"Mr. and Mrs. McMeri," Dr. Jennings began. "I've analyzed the results. They have confirmed your suspicions—your daughter is deaf."

Elliana felt like her insides were made of glass—and everything shattered. Though the doctor moved his mouth with the words she expected, they would not permeate her mind. She licked her cracked lips, even though her tongue was dry, and spoke.

"How bad?"

Dr. Jennings gave her a sympathetic look before continuing. There was a significant lag between his words and the McMeris' response. Finally, Elliana tasted the bitter words: Christa was profoundly hearing impaired with a "corner audiogram." This meant that Christa responded only to very loud, low tones.

Dr. Jennings elaborated on the diagnosis. "Your daughter's hearing loss is so profound that she may not be able to communicate orally. Do not expect her to call you 'Mommy' or 'Daddy.'" He spoke gently but he looked into their eyes gravely.

It tore Elliana apart. Holding back her tears, she replied defiantly. "My baby will be able to talk just like everyone else. She will call me 'Mommy' just like everyone else." She surprised herself with the vehemence in her own voice.

Mitch rested his hand on her back and stroked her soothingly. He looked at his wife, his eyes brimming with tears, but his voice was strong when he turned to the doctor to get more information.

"What do you think caused this?"

"I know this is difficult and you will want to place blame somewhere. But the cause is unknown. Sometimes it just happens." Dr. Jennings leaned back in his chair. He appeared to want to be anywhere but there—he was a man who wore his heart on his sleeve, even after all the years. "I don't pretend to know what this is like. But there are many support groups who do." He pulled out a brochure about sensorineural hearing loss.

Mitch took it from the doctor. Elliana glanced over and saw pictures of women smiling. *What on earth?* she thought.

She was almost offended. There was nothing happy about the situation, and the smiling model on the brochure seemed to mock their situation.

Elliana trudged zombie-like across the parking lot. The sun was shining and the birds were singing—a gorgeous spring day. *Why does the whole world appear so inappropriate, so indifferent?* Elliana thought.

On the way home, the anger turned from the doctor to nature, to herself. *Did I do something wrong while I was pregnant?*

She fiddled with her wedding ring on her finger and stared absentmindedly at the highway. In and out of awareness, Elliana retreated within herself further. *Why did I work until the month before the due date? Maybe I should've taken time off…maybe the stressful commute did something to her.* Gritting her teeth, Elliana tried to swallow back tears as she thought, *I should have quit my job sooner.*

The McMeris were home before they remembered that they had to pick up Jadelynn from their neighbor Joanna. Mitch had to collect himself before he did so; he spent a moment alone in the bedroom while Elliana sat and stared at her daughter. She was blissfully unaware of the conflict, but not of her surroundings. Her bright eyes reflected alertness and engagement with the sights around her. Just looking at her, no one would ever have guessed she was… deaf.

The guilt was relentless. Having exhausted all other possibilities for Christa's condition, Elliana began looking at the situation on a grander scale. *Is God punishing me for something I did in the past?* The realization then crashed into her like a tidal wave: all the music she played for Christa while she was in the womb—all the times she wrapped her headphones around the crest of her belly—was in vain. All the songs she lovingly sang to the life inside her fell on ears that would never hear the magic of melody. The bright future of her baby turned dark and gray like a storm cloud. Suddenly there was a long stretch of doubt and uncertainty on the horizon.

Were they mourning for their daughter's deafness? Or were they mourning for their dashed dream of the "perfect child"? The only part of the situation that was more difficult than accepting the truth was revealing it to the family and their friends. She would receive support, but seeing their reactions would be like feeling the harsh sting of the diagnosis all over.

"I don't know how I'll do it," Elliana whispered after Mitch made the call to his parents.

He looked at her sympathetically before saying, "I will." After a pause, he added, "After all, my mom will be the most affected."

"I don't doubt that."

"But look at her…" Mitch gestured to Christa sitting up on her own beside Jadelynn, who was having tummy time. The two sisters looked at each other thoughtfully and then one would make a funny face. Elliana felt a fish hook tugging at her heart and emotionally pulling her toward them.

"What?" she asked. "What about her?"

"The way she's interacting with Jadelynn. She's still a normal baby. She still communicates with her, and she's still so young. If she can do it now, she will be able to later."

The words did nothing to assuage Elliana's despair; they may as well have fallen upon deaf ears.

FLIPPING

✧ ✧ ✧

"Everyone, we have some news," Mitch said, sitting at the head of the table during dinner. He was unsmiling, which caused his family to look at him questioningly. Elliana sat beside him and stared at her plate of half-eaten homemade Italian spaghetti and meatballs. The weight of eight pairs of eyes oppressed her.

Mitch continued after sighing. "We have had some... some concerns about Christa's health." A pin could have fallen in that silence, and it rattled them to the core. "Elliana investigated those suspicions. Finally, the audiologist confirmed her worries: Christa is deaf."

Questions didn't explode into the air. Instead, gravity felt heavier, somehow.

Mitch's oldest brother, Allan, spoke up first. "How?" His face looked older as he looked to Mitch in sympathy for his daughter.

"The doctors don't know," said Mitch. "It could be a prenatal illness, trauma during the birth or after, a virus, something genetic, mutation..."

Mitch's mother looked toward Elliana. "We don't have a family history of deafness." Her voice was weak but her gaze was piercing.

"Mom," Allan said pointedly, "having a special-needs child is not a crime, a sin, or anything to be ashamed of." His eldest had just been diagnosed with ADHD.

Elliana pushed her food around on the plate. "How did this happen?" was a question she wanted answers to as well. Ever since they'd gotten the diagnosis, she'd been beating herself up, wondering if she'd done something—or *not* done something—that caused Christa's hearing loss.

But now, hearing the question from someone else, she suddenly realized it was the wrong question to be asking. Looking backward would never get them where they needed to go. She had to stop focusing on how it happened and start figuring out what to do about it. She had to start reconfiguring her questions to, "How can I make sure Christa's deafness doesn't limit her? That she doesn't feel inferior? That she has opportunities and experiences success?"

Elliana looked around the table at the stricken faces that reflected all the shock, pain, and sorrow she had been feeling. But instead of being consoled, something inside her rebelled. Elliana lifted her chin and looked Mitch's mother straight in the eye.

"I know it's a shock and of course it is upsetting. But it's not an insurmountable tragedy. She isn't dying; her life isn't over. Christa has a strong body, a good mind, and a loving family. She has everything she needs to have a wonderful life. I don't want any of us giving her the idea that she is a poor victim or 'less than'—and that includes me!"

Everyone stared at her in surprise; they weren't used to such forcefulness. Mitch took her hand and squeezed it.

"You're right," said Allan's wife, Nina. "Everyone's got challenges. It all depends on how you deal with them if they define your life or not."

For the first time since the diagnosis, Elliana felt hopeful, empowered. She had to be strong for everyone—her husband, her family, and, most importantly, her daughter, who needed her more than ever.

✤ ✤ ✤

Elliana's high didn't last long. The next day, things seemed nearly as dark and dismal as before. Sometimes she felt resolute and declared that the experience would teach her family new lessons on determination and strength. Then it was like someone had removed a queen of spades from the bottom of a house of cards—everything seemed to fall around her.

On one of her "bad" days, Elliana heard the sweeping rescendos and feverish notes of Beethoven's "Symphony No. 5" in the living room. The urgent and agitated first movement was juxtaposed with the sudden booms of the tympani, drum, and fierce strings. The music reflected Elliana's oscillating emotions.

Elliana walked into the living room with a babbling Jadelynn in her arms. Seeing Christa and her daddy next to the blasting CD player, she stalked over and turned the volume down.

"What on earth are you doing?" she asked.

"Beethoven was deaf, you know," said Mitch.

"Everyone knows that Beethoven was deaf," Elliana snapped.

"But listen to what he was able to do," Mitch said.

Perhaps it was Mitch's defense mechanism, but he overcompensated Elliana's somber determination with overblown optimism. Most of the time it reassured her, but sometimes—like today—it just set her teeth on edge, like he was ignoring the full gravity of the situation.

"He also became deaf as an adult," she replied flatly. "It's different."

"Yes, but wouldn't that also make it harder to adjust to a new world? And he still managed to find and create beauty in it."

Elliana rolled her eyes.

But the next day when Mitch was at work, she picked up the book he was reading: *The Story of My Life* by Helen Keller. An educator, journalist, and humanitarian, she suffered the loss of two senses—hearing *and* vision—and yet, managed to do more in a lifetime than most people with full capabilities.

"And how did it all begin?" Elliana thought aloud. "With a good teacher."

That's it, Elliana thought. *That's what we need.* A baby's brain was a very malleable structure, and surely if they got her the right teachers early in life, she could compensate for whatever deficits she had. Access to a quality education would be where Christa's success story would begin.

Endless pamphlets, brochures, and printouts infiltrated the living room. "Deaf culture" was brand-new to all of them, and Elliana realized she was stepping into another world. Having an acquaintance familiar with that experience would have been a lifesaver, but no one in their circle could help them out.

With Mitch working long hours, the bulk of the research fell to Elliana. And that often meant simply thumping down the yellow pages and grabbing a phone.

"Hi, I'm Elliana McMeri. I heard you have a Deaf program?"

But she wasn't content just hearing about what they had to offer; she wanted to see for herself. It wasn't easy to hustle two babies into her little Honda Civic, diaper bags and all, but she visited every single place on the list.

"What sorts of sign languages did you have in mind? Here we teach ASL, the most common," said one of the principals as they strolled down the halls of a potential school candidate.

"There are different types?" Elliana felt ignorant.

The principal nodded patiently. "Yes. There's American Sign Language, or ASL, then Signing Exact English...among others, but they're the most common."

This is getting overwhelming. But Elliana glanced at her wide-eyed cherub and felt emboldened.

The Deaf community was far from cohesive, she would discover. Aside from signing, there were also oral options — somewhat controversial among different Deaf enclaves. Elliana listened to one interpreter make sense of her impassioned deaf client, who was staunchly against it. There were many opinions, some inflammatory, and no "one-size-fits-all" answer.

"Total communication" trained deaf kids to use both sign and talk simultaneously. And then there was the famous option. The John Tracy Clinic in downtown L.A. was established by none other than actor Spencer Tracy and his wife. Their deaf son inspired them to pave a way for him to live as normal a life as he could. One of the golden opportunities to do that? Lip reading.

"You might try this oral school in the city of Whittier," mentioned one of the nurses at the pediatrician's office during one of Christa's checkups. "It's inside a church."

Elliana was on it. Several wrong turns later, she stumbled inside the church. A kind-faced lady with mousy brown hair greeted her.

"I'm so glad you came to visit — these kids can show you so much." They passed by one of the classrooms. "Boys and girls, pay attention and listen to the music. Move your body and dance with the music." Elliana recognized the music from one of the Wee Sing tapes. Five kids, around three to four years old, were following the classroom teacher in spirited dance. They kicked their little legs, wiggled their bodies, waved their arms, and giggled. "Are you listening to the music?"

And from there she let the children, the living testimonies of the school's effectiveness, do the literal talking. One boy with short blond hair of about age six was en route to the back door. They flagged him down.

"Introduce yourself," the instructor, Jean, gently requested.

All Elliana could see was his Spider-Man backpack. He turned away from Jean and faced Elliana with confidence.

"Hi, I'm David. I'm in the first grade." His speech was not perfect, but easily understood, and he did not have the typical throaty voice.

She jumped back. With a face brightened with shock, she faced Jean and wanted to exclaim, *Is he really deaf?*

Jean's face crinkled into a smile. He *was* deaf. He just had the most beautiful voice—one could barely, if ever, distinguish that he was deaf. The only giveaway was the device in his ear.

"Wow," Elliana finally replied. "Do you like it here?"

He shrugged. "I like recess." Jean tapped him on the arm playfully before letting him go.

Elliana was still under the spell of that little boy's voice. "So… they can hear?"

"Well, he has hearing aids. How old is your little one?"

"Fifteen months."

"I'm glad to hear it. It's easier when they start young. Let me tell you all about the infant program," she added. "We do not emphasize lip reading at all. Teachers actually cover their mouths with a piece of paper during the speech section so kids can learn to speak by listening with whatever residual hearing they have."

Even as she spoke, Elliana couldn't get the image of the little boy with the Spider-Man backpack out of her mind. And he was so… normal. Not that the other kids weren't, but he could slip through life in the hearing world. It was surely challenging, but his chance of being a part of mainstream community seemed much brighter. She imagined his life: hearing his siblings' laughs, the sound of gleeful screams on the playground during his favorite part of school, and yes, music.

The image of Mitch flashed across her mind — waving his arms around triumphantly during his favorite portions of his favorite symphonies. The sight alone was enough to make her heart swell, but the accompanying music was something she heartily appreciated too. Ultimately, she wanted Christa to acknowledge that there was something called "music." Not just to name it, but to experience it.

That's when Elliana knew she had made her decision.

⁜ ⁜ ⁜

Everything happened so quickly. Christa was fitted with gigantic hearing aids, which dwarfed her little ears so much that they had to use surgical tape and loops to secure them.

Christa attended the program twice a week, with Elliana supplementing her auditory-oral training at home. She lined up all of Christa's toys on the dining room table, Christa next to her on one side and Jadelynn on the other.

They took turns to play: "Airplane goes Aa, Aa," waving the little toy airplane on the air; "Rabbit goes hop, hop, hop," the little rabbit scurrying across the table; "Cow goes moo, moo, moo…"

They played the game several times a day, with Jean's words in the back of her mind: "Talk to her constantly and show her the sources of all sounds."

"Listen, water is running," Elliana told Christa as she prepared her bath.

"Listen to the bird tweeting."

"Walk. Walk, walk… let's walk down to the bedroom!"

She was narrating her life to her daughter. "I feel like I have verbal diarrhea," she confessed to Mitch. They exchanged a rare devilish smile.

One day, Elliana was busy preparing the dinner and she heard Jadelynn pick up the toy airplane. Elliana turned her face toward her daughters and saw Jadelynn looking at Christa.

"Airplane goes Aa, Aa, Aa." Jadelynn was six months younger than Christa. Elliana gulped and silently prayed.

Please let Christa register what she hears and talk soon.

Mitch grabbed each of his little girls and sat them on either side of him. They wiggled impatiently until he dropped his fingers on the ivory keys, smudged from so much use.

"Every good boy does fine." He recited the mnemonic for the notes and hoped his girls would catch on. Christa and Jadelynn's jaws fell open as they watched their father glide across the keys. As a music teacher, he wanted to share the beauty of music with his girls, and desperately wanted Christa to know the phenomenon existed at all.

But she was making progress. At that point she had had

auditory-oral training for over a year. With her mother's and her schoolteachers' efforts, she learned to listen to everyday environmental sounds:

"Listen, the bird is singing."

"Listen, the telephone is ringing."

"Listen, the water is running."

Christa acquired some vocabulary and simple sentences with time. However, she was unable to hear all the sounds even with the most powerful hearing aids; her audiogram showed that more than half of the sounds fell off the "speech banana," or range of human hearing.

After Mitch played a few songs, Christa looked up at him with her ever-questioning eyes. She pushed the far-right end of the piano keys with her chubby fingers.

"Broken?" she asked, tilting her head.

After attending the auditory-oral school for more than one year, teachers raised the possibility of cochlear implants.

"The FDA approved cochlear implants in the early 1990s for children with prelingual severe to profound sensorineural hearing loss in both ears. Honestly, there have been an incredible amount of success stories since then," assured Christa's teacher. "Think of hearing aids like a built-in remote control—they increase the volume of sounds. A cochlear implant moves past the ear damage so stimulations will reach the auditory nerve."

Ever the optimist, Mitch was captivated by the possibilities the amazing new technology offered. "Can you imagine?" he said. "She'll even be able to hear the high tone of the music!"

But Elliana couldn't get her mind off the dangers. Every surgery has complications. What if something went wrong? Was she risking too much to try to make Christa "normal"?

FLIPPING

Standing at the crossroads again. Another decision to make. Knowing their decision now would affect their little girl's life forever. *God, please help us make the right one.*

Christa was referred to House Ear Institute in downtown Los Angeles for an evaluation and received favorable news. Her primary physician and the specialist had collaborated in a painstaking process to secure the insurance company's approval for the procedure. With Christa's doctors and now even the insurance company on board, they decided to take the plunge.

As the holiday season approached, the McMeris found it difficult to focus on the joys and the rituals of the season. The necessary medical examinations for Christa's cochlear implant dominated their time. Only after their daughter emerged safe and sound (and dare they say hearing?) could they proceed with the future.

Their surgeon, Dr. Bill, tall and slim with gray hair, a classy gentleman, explained the procedure to the family slowly: twenty-two segments of electrodes would be inserted into her cochlea. A receiver would then be secured in the bone behind the ear, underneath the skin. Once the wound healed, about one month after the surgical date, the processor—similar to a computer's—would be programmed so all internal and external pieces smoothly worked together. Then, Christa could hear the sound. His smile was encouraging.

Though the surgeon had a deep, soothing voice that quelled Elliana and Mitch's anxiety to some degree, the idea of such an invasive surgery on their daughter was frightening. *Open a hole on her skull and insert a wire into her head, and put a magnet on her bone underneath the skin...*

"Let me just emphasize one point," Dr. Bill said, holding up his index finger. "This isn't all up to one player. While

Christa will have the capability of hearing after this procedure, this still isn't a magical, flick-of-the-wand solution. Yes, she'll have the capability and the right hardware. But she will also need to develop the skill with the proper training—she must develop her 'software,' if you will." His eyes lingered on Christa, looking around in her father's lap. "The team effort is vital. Christa's success will only come when the surgeons, speech therapists, audiologists, and particularly the family are willing to work together."

"That's no problem," said Mitch. "We would build a tower to the moon with our bare hands if it meant she would be better off!"

"I know you can't make our decision for us," said Elliana. "But what would you do? If it was your daughter?"

"I would do it," Dr. Bill replied without hesitation. "There are risks as there are with any procedure. Honestly, not every hearing impaired is a good candidate for the cochlear implant. I have thoroughly evaluated Christa's case and I am confident this procedure will bring the positive outcome to her future. To answer your question, if it were my daughter, I'd accept the risk because I've seen firsthand what a difference it can make."

Exchanging a look, Elliana and Mitch came to a wordless agreement.

"That's good enough for us," Mitch said.

✢ ✢ ✢

Later that night, Elliana tucked both girls into bed. "Christa has a big day coming soon," she explained, pulling the blankets up to Jadelynn's neck. "Christa is getting her ears fixed so she can hear better."

"Ears?" Jadelynn asked, pointing at her own ear.

"That's right! Ears!" Elliana said, playfully flicking her earlobe.

With all the attention on Christa, she hoped she hadn't been neglecting the little two-year-old. *I've got to make sure to carve out some one-on-one time with her,* she thought.

Then she looked over at Christa, who was looking at the glow-in-the-dark star stickers on the ceiling, a peaceful, faraway smile on her face. Nothing seemed to vex her. It was a trait Elliana hoped that Christa could maintain into the next stage of her life…

She would need it.

✤ ✤ ✤

It was four days before Christmas, and all through the McMeri house was pre-surgery anxiety.

On the morning of the surgical date, the hospital drive was quiet, with everyone still groggy from lack of sleep. Once they made it to the waiting room, Christa sank sleepily into Mitch's lap while Elliana attended to all the paperwork for the surgery.

"May I have your insurance card, ma'am?" The lady at the desk wearing a Santa hat made a copy of the insurance card—even though insurance had authorized the procedure, she insisted on having it on file anyway.

The tree at the corner of the waiting room was decorated with gold-and-silver tinsel. Mitch felt his heartbeat drum three times faster than the blinking lights and wished he felt as cheerful.

FLIPPING

A nurse wearing teal scrubs led them into an exam room. Two nurses coordinated, attaching electrodes onto Christa's skin to monitor her vitals, inserting needles into her veins, shaving the right side of her head to prepare for the invasion. Elliana held Christa's hands and wouldn't let go until she had to.

A woman came to the room with a release form. "It's just routine," she assured them.

The paperwork stated:

The risks and benefits associated with the procedure have been explained to me. However, I understand there is no certainty that I will achieve these benefits and no guarantee has been made to me regarding the outcome of the procedure(s).

I also authorize the administration of sedation and/or anesthesia as may be deemed advisable or necessary for my comfort, well-being, and safety.

The risks and possible undesirable consequences associated with the procedure have been explained to me including, but not limited to, blood loss, transfusion reactions, infection, heart complications, blood clots, loss of or loss of use of body parts, neurological injury or death.

Not very comforting, but they signed it anyway. Before they knew it, it was time for Christa to be transported to her surgery. She looked so little on the gurney as she disappeared behind the big steel doors of the hospital. The next time they saw Christa, she'd be brand-new with her bionic ear.

✢ ✢ ✢

God, Elliana prayed, *please be present in the room with these surgeons. Use your almighty power.*

Elliana's clammy hands remained tightly clasped together as she stared at the TV. There was a big snowstorm in the northeast. Though there was no snow in Southern California, Elliana felt an icy-cold sensation in her spine. Mitch intuitively came over and handed her a paper cup of hot coffee. She took it but even the steam from the hot liquid could not ease her shivering.

The morning passed by far too slowly. No matter how she tried to distract herself, all she could think of was the hole the doctors were cutting in her baby's skull. None of her terror abated until their messenger finally arrived.

"So? How did it go?" they asked in unison.

The nurse didn't beat around the bush. "The surgery went well. She's still asleep."

Elliana sighed with relief, but she knew she couldn't fully calm down until she saw Christa herself. They followed the nurse to the recovery room. However, seeing the jungle of tubes attached to Christa's smooth arm, and machines humming and blipping around her, Elliana felt anything but comforted.

"It's okay, she'll come out of this better than ever. Just remember that," Mitch reassured her, stroking his wife's arm. They anticipated their daughter's awakening with racing minds and hopeful hearts.

When she finally opened her eyes, her parents were right beside her.

"How are you feeling, champ?" Mitch asked.

Elliana wondered what Christa heard.

Chapter 6

Four weeks after the surgery, Christa was ready for the first mapping for her cochlear implant. Elliana took Jadelynn to the babysitter's. Jadelynn's face crinkled. The threat of a tantrum loomed.

Elliana felt horribly guilty for leaving her with the sitter again. But the day was an important one. Their audiologist would explain the mapping process to them.

"We won't take long, sweetie," said Elliana, giving Jadelynn a quick hug before darting out the door.

"Glad to see you," greeted Becky, the audiologist in Dr. Bill's office. She appeared to be in her late thirties, with a stylish, short haircut. She bent down and smiled wide to Christa, who looked at her with distrust. "Let's get mapping, shall we? We'll play a game while working on that."

The mapping process involved connecting the twenty-two internal electrode segments in Christa's head to the external piece, the small computer.

"During the mapping process, I'll determine the minimum volume where Christa can hear sound. Then we'll do the same with maximum volume for her to hear comfortably for each electrode." She paused and gave a wan smile. "I won't lie, this is not the *easiest* task for a two-and-a-half-year-old."

"What if it doesn't work the first time...what if it's inaccurate?" Elliana asked, looking down at her toddler dubiously.

"This first mapping is a 'conditioning play.' It can be adjusted if necessary in a month's time, during our follow-up. We'll follow her closely in the first year."

"And I suppose I'll have to pay attention to Christa's response to the sound."

"Right," Becky affirmed.

Christa tugged Elliana's pant leg and held up her arms to be picked up.

"It's okay, honey," Elliana said. "We're going to stay here for a while. But I'll be with you the whole time. We're going to play a game. Okay?"

As positive as she was on the outside, inside, Elliana was filled with uncertainty. She was overwhelmed by all the instructions on how to take care of the processer and external portion of the implant. And she wondered if they'd underestimated the demands of the training that was involved. She wasn't a teacher. Would she be able to teach Christa everything she needed to know? And if she couldn't, would the cochlear implant even benefit Christa at all?

❖ ❖ ❖

During the next few weeks, it seemed that the previously calm baby—the envy of the entire extended McMeri clan—had been replaced with another child entirely. Christa was prone to either sudden fits or endless bouts of whining and fussing. She awoke to a world that had eluded her. But now Christa faced the full, untamed ferocity of sound…and she didn't know how to handle it.

Nor did Elliana. She was helpless.

The splash of water. The low buzz of the air conditioner. The whir of a fan. The distant calls of birds. Every sound, big or small, was an alarming mystery to solve immediately. Christa would suddenly jerk, trying to identify the source of a sound. Sometimes she broke into a sprint out of fear. Other times she tiptoed around, slightly tilting her head toward the air, as if she were following an aural trail.

The lawn mower was unbearable. Jadelynn's banging on the piano keys transformed a previous source of intrigue into a white-fanged monster. Speech was no longer soothing—it had warped what had once been the beloved act of her family's innocuous mouth movements and kind facial expressions. Now noise exploded from their mouths.

"What's dat?" Christa would ask suddenly.

"It's water boiling," Elliana said, picking up her daughter and holding her a little distance away from the bubbling water of the steaming pot.

But Christa scrunched up her nose and groaned. "No!"

Christa whimpered and cried in frustration. There were so many sounds that it was hard for Elliana to home in on the one that had grabbed Christa's attention.

"Her world is probably overwhelming," Elliana said softly to Mitch as they lay together side by side in bed. She was drained from the day, but she knew that Christa's mental exhaustion had to be something else entirely. "There is so much noise coming at her, and she has no idea what any of it means. All these sounds with the cochlear implant must be much more powerful and foreign to her compared to her hearing aids previously. I wish I could hear what she hears."

"It's all new. But she'll pick it up soon enough. Just give it time," Mitch said.

"I know," she replied. "Are we doing a good job? Christa needs so much attention, I feel like I'm ignoring Jadelynn."

"You're doing an *amazing* job. With both the girls. It makes me tired just thinking about all you do!"

Mitch turned to kiss his wife, only to find that poor Elliana had fallen into a deep slumber beside him—lips parted, arm still lazily stretched across the bed, as if to flip the lamp switch. He smiled and reached over her to turn off the light.

✣ ✣ ✣

But the wins soon came. For five rigorous mornings per week, Christa continued her auditory-oral training at her school.

"January. February. March. April." The teacher covered the calendar names with sheets of blank paper to force the students to listen for the missing information.

In six months, Christa started to make sounds that she couldn't before receiving the cochlear implant, like *sh* and *guh*. She started hearing telephone rings. But the biggest win of all happened with Mitch.

"Daddy," Christa said energetically, tugging on his shirt.

When he looked down, he saw his daughter continuing to pull on his shirt as she guided him... toward the piano.

"What is it?" he asked.

Christa bowed her wired head and repeatedly hit the rightmost side of the piano ivories. Mitch heard the tinkling of the high pitches and searched Christa's little round face. It lit up with delight.

"What is it, sweetie?" he asked again.

FLIPPING

Christa turned up and gave him a toothy grin. "They are okay now."

Jadelynn stood nearby as an unnoticed observer. She suddenly appeared by her father and looked up at him. "Christa loves music."

With that, Mitch lifted his dark-rimmed glasses and pressed his finger pads against the corners of his eyes. He didn't know how he'd explain such an emotion to them.

With time, the dynamic changed in the house. Jadelynn and Christa fought like typical young siblings, but Jadelynn always piped up as the voice of her sister. She clarified her frustrations and also interpreted whenever Christa couldn't understand the world around her.

"Wah, wah," she made her baby doll cry, which caused Christa to cock her head. Jadelynn patiently put down her doll—which they had only just been fighting over—and laced her fingers over her knees. "That's the sound babies make, Christa. When they want their mommies."

It warmed their hearts to see Jadelynn talking as slowly as possible around her sister and giving long-winded, sometimes hilariously inaccurate, explanations. Their family was not perfect, but they dearly loved one another. That love would sustain them for years to come.

⁜ ⁜ ⁜

When Elliana went to parent-teacher night at the auditory oral deaf school, she was thrilled to hear that Christa was excelling both socially and academically. She had plenty of friends, always participated in class, and her language skills were improving.

"The only thing I've noticed," said her teacher Mrs. Joyce,

"is that she can be a bit of a wiggle worm in class if we're not involved in some kind of activity. She has a hard time sitting still."

"She's always had a lot of energy," Elliana said. "At home she's always out riding her bike or climbing a tree. Jadelynn's content to play inside all day, but Christa's a real tomboy." She swallowed hard. "You don't think she's...abnormally hyperactive, do you? Her cousin has ADHD..."

"Oh, no, nothing like that," Mrs. Joyce said. "People are so quick to see attention-deficit these days. I think she's probably a kinesthetic learner. Have you thought about enrolling her in dance or gymnastics? Lots of kids start joining sports teams about now."

No doubt Mrs. Joyce could see the huge exclamation mark fly above Elliana's head. "Don't you think with her condition it's a little risky?" But then she realized perhaps there was a reason Mrs. Joyce had suggested only non-team sports.

✤ ✤ ✤

Elliana took the girls to the YMCA of Torrance for their first class. Slender instructors coached rubber-limbed children who were effortlessly bending into pretzel shapes at will. Elliana's heart almost stopped when she saw a little girl of about Christa's age sprinting and cartwheeling across the mat.

Christa was riveted.

"Hi there," Elliana ventured, extending a hand to the instructor, Ms. Sharyn. "I'm Elliana and these are my daughters, Jadelynn and Christa. I just wanted to let you know...Christa wears a processor for her cochlear implant. It amplifies the sounds around her, besides voices, and she might get distracted by all the background noises. Could you try staying closer to her and facing her when helping her?"

The fresh-faced instructor didn't miss a beat. "Sure. I work with many special-needs children. If there's anything else you'd like us to do, please do let us know."

"Okay, let's go! Let's go!" Christa looked like she'd explode from her willingness to try doing the "cool moves" like the other kids.

Elliana looked down and stroked Christa's blond hair. "Easy, there," she said with a smile. "You won't be doing flips in one day!"

"Oh yeah?"

Elliana watched from the edge of the gym as the class started.

Christa listened intently to the instructor but bounced impatiently while doing so. The instructor did as Elliana requested and always stood by and faced Christa unless she was helping another student. Seeing that, Elliana relaxed.

"Mommy, I love it, I love it!" Christa cried as they drove home. Soon, she and Jadelynn were in and out of the YMCA on a regular basis. They greeted the girl at the reception desk like an old friend. Christa would have lived at the gym if she could.

At five years old, Jadelynn enjoyed the classes, but Christa truly blossomed. The focus she had would have been remarkable for someone twice her age. She would watch the instructor intently as she demonstrated the new move, as if committing it to memory. She seemed determined to get it right the first time; and often she did.

She quickly became the star of the class and, despite her imperfect speaking skills, a leader too. Even the older girls looked up to her and would come to her for help with their moves and routines. The girls had a language of form and movement beyond the spoken word.

Gymnastics was also Christa's bridge to the hearing world outside the gym. Whenever anyone came over, she just shot them a grin and showed off her new tricks: back walkovers, handstands, splits, spider walks, and anything new she learned in class that week.

"She likes to greet people with gymnastics moves," Elliana would tell her friends with a laugh.

Watching her little girl effortlessly cartwheel across the gym floor, Elliana marveled that she'd ever worried Christa wouldn't be able to keep up.

That year, Christa completed Level 3.

She passed Level 4 right after her sixth birthday.

✤ ✤ ✤

Not long afterward, Christa's instructor at the Y, Mrs. Sharyn, came over to Elliana after the class. "Christa had a great workout today," she said. "She really gave it a hundred percent."

"I have to," piped up Christa, "if I'm going to make it to Level Five and Six and Seven and…!"

Elliana and Mrs. Sharyn exchanged a smile.

"That reminds me," said Mrs. Sharyn. "There is something I wanted to speak to you about."

Elliana sent Christa skipping off to practice her straddle jump with Jadelynn. "I hope neither of the girls has been giving you grief," she said when Christa was out of earshot.

Ms. Sharyn's green eyes twinkled. "Oh, no. Quite the contrary. They're both a joy to work with. But Christa's really excelling. Not only does she have natural talent, but she's got unusual drive too. It's a rare combination. Have you ever considered maybe enrolling her in ENA Gymnastics?"

"What's that?"

"Well, I would venture to say our little class here is a chance for kids to have fun and work out. But I don't know if we can help Christa reach her full potential. ENA Gymnastics and Dance Academy—they can prepare Christa for the major leagues."

Elliana was thrilled that Christa was doing so well, but she hated the idea of taking her out of the Y. That was the only real social circle she had left. But she didn't want anything holding Christa back from chasing her passion. If she really wanted to pursue gymnastics, Elliana would do everything she could to help her succeed.

When she told Christa about Mrs. Sharyn's proposal, her daughter didn't give it a second thought.

"Can I? Can I go? *Please?* I want to be the best gymnast ever!"

Jadelynn broke in. "Mom, I don't want to be in the major leagues. I don't have to go, do I?"

"Of course not, honey. It's entirely up to you. It's great that you and Christa share so many things, but you don't have to do everything together."

The very next day Elliana went to the ENA Academy to get a feel for the place. And it was rigorous—she knew it as soon as she walked in. Awards and trophies lined the hallway. In the gym, there was a seriousness in the air, a concentrated determination on the gymnasts' faces. Instead of the laughter and chatter that filled the Y, the only sound was the crack of the uneven bars and the thump of girls sticking their landings.

Elliana had read that the academy was founded and run by Eugene Wilson, who wanted to build a top-notch facility for true devotees of the sport he loved so much. He and his wife, Agnes, were previous national gymnastics champions.

Eugene himself boasted a World Cup master championship and had earned over twenty international medals from various competitions.

Elliana saw Coach Eugene on the other side of the gym. His face froze in observation as a gnarled tree, watching a girl practice a back handspring from a back walkover on the four-inch-wide balance beam.

"No, no," he called out when the girl jumped down from the beam. "Do you remember this lesson? What'd I say about posture here?"

Elliana felt her shoulders rise in empathetic defensiveness for the pupil. Still, she could tell Coach Eugene knew his stuff. Right after the student performed the move correctly, he high-fived her. He seemed to have rigorous, but not impossible, expectations.

Just then he glanced around and saw Elliana. Within seconds he swished over in his windbreaker and pumped her hand with a strong handshake. His face crinkled into a warm smile. "Hello, hello! You must be Mrs. McMeri."

"Elliana, please."

"So I understand your daughter is a promising young gymnast?"

"Yes, she's a regular little monkey. She seems to progress rapidly, and the Y says she's outgrowing what they can offer her. They suggested she come here."

"Excellent! We'd be glad to have her if she's ready to do

what it takes to make it to the next level. You are aware of the program requirements, right? Practice five days a week and Saturdays plus meets. It isn't for the faint-hearted. We're looking for total dedication."

"I understand," said Elliana. "Christa lives and breathes gymnastics. I think she'll fit right in. Oh, and one thing you should know is that Christa is deaf—"

The smile on Coach Eugene's face froze and he took a step backward.

Elliana felt the blood rush from her face. "She wears a processor for her cochlear implant," she rushed to explain, "so you can communicate with her just fine. It doesn't hold her back at all."

But she could tell he was no longer listening.

"I'm afraid I don't think we can offer her a place here," he said. "This is a special training program. We have limited spaces. I have to focus on the athletes who have a chance to go all the way to Elite. We're training national champions and Olympic hopefuls."

"But, who's to say Christa can't go all the way? She—"

The coach cut her off. "I'm sorry. This just isn't the right program for her. But there are plenty of other high-caliber gyms in the area that I'm sure would be happy to work with her."

"But... you're the best!"

"I'm sorry. If you'll excuse me, I'm afraid I have to get back to practice."

He left Elliana staring after him. She had never felt so furious in her life. She turned on her heel and stormed out. That evening she unloaded on Mitch.

"Who is he to say how far she can go without even *seeing* her?" she hissed, careful not to let the girls overhear. "That arrogant, close-minded jerk! I'll tell you what we're going to do. We're going to find another gym, and we'll rub his nose in it when she beats his girls in competition. Then we'll see who has the last laugh!"

"Sounds like a plan, Mama Bear," said Mitch. She allowed him to coax a reluctant smile out of her, but inside she was still fuming. *No one was going to stand in the way of her baby's passion. Not if she had anything to do with it.*

The next day, she looked up all the other gyms in town and visited every single one of them. Most of them were nice, with friendly, knowledgeable instructors. But none of them compared to the Academy in terms of rigor, expertise, or proven results. It was clearly in a league of its own. If Christa was going to shoot for the stars, there was only one place for her to go.

The next day, after their class at the Y, Elliana took the girls to the Academy. "Now don't be nervous," Elliana told Christa. Her eyes were big as half-dollars as she took it all in.

"They're *good*," Christa whispered, a mix of envy and hope in her voice.

Elliana's heart contracted. *This has to work.*

She carefully waited until the girl Coach Eugene was training finished her double layout dismount off the uneven bars.

"Okay, let's go," she said. Taking her daughter by the hand, she quickly strode into the middle of the gym.

"Coach Eugene!"

He turned to look and he clearly wasn't happy to see her.

"Mrs. McMeri, I told you —"

"I know what you said. But I wanted you to meet my daughter. I'd like you to tell her directly what you told me."

The coach frowned, a range of emotions playing across

his face. Guilt, sympathy, anger for being put in this position...

Elliana could tell he wasn't a cold or unfeeling man. His life's work was making aspiring gymnasts' dreams come true, not crushing them. This would be hard for him—if he could bring himself to do it.

He knelt down, speaking a little louder and slower than usual. "Your mom tells me you are quite a good gymnast. And I am sure you are. But this gym is for, uh, we only have a limited number of spaces and..." Suddenly he stopped, his attention caught by something over her shoulder.

"Jessica, who's that?" he called to his assistant, his gaze still transfixed by the girl on the floor mat performing a series of high-flying back handsprings, front walkovers, leaps, jumps, and flips.

"*That* is my daughter Christa," said Elliana triumphantly. "This is my *other* daughter, Jadelynn."

He didn't take his eyes off Christa, who was now in a perfect handstand. She tucked her head, rolled out the handstand, and went into an elegant dance routine. Even without a soundtrack, her graceful leaps and pirouettes made you hear the music that wasn't there.

When she finished, her body collapsed into a tiny ball, Coach Eugene slowly turned back to Elliana, his expression unreadable.

Elliana held her breath.

"You tricked me," he finally said.

Elliana gave an uncertain half-smile. "You deserved it."

His eyebrows shot up in surprise. "Well now," he said, his face breaking into a grin, "I guess I did."

✦ ✦ ✦

FLIPPING

Christa was thrilled to start at the Academy, never knowing how close she came to not getting in. She was determined to catch up to the other girls, and she threw everything she had into her training. At home, she would practice for hours in the backyard or the living room, which she'd convinced her parents to convert into a home gym. Seeing how hard she worked, how much she wanted to please her coach, pulled at Elliana's heartstrings.

But she also noticed a change come over her daughter. Gone was the free-spirited, fun-loving girl who would launch into a spontaneous song-and-dance routine or start a belching competition with her sister. This new Christa was quieter, more somber and serious. Was this just a natural maturing out of the unselfconscious ebullience of childhood? Or was she *too* focused for a girl her age?

❖ ❖ ❖

At the end of Christa's first-grade year, her teacher gave her a glowing report.

"She's doing so well," Mrs. Joyce said, "we think she is ready to be mainstreamed full time next year."

Elliana felt a cold lump of anxiety in her stomach. "Are you sure?" She felt safe and secure in this auditory-oral school; it almost seemed like a cruel punishment to reward Christa's success by taking her away from her friends and beloved teachers.

"Our goal is preparing the students here to be a part of society," Mrs. Joyce reminded Elliana. "Christa's ready for the next step now."

"Maybe one more year?" Elliana asked. "Her language

still isn't perfect."

"This is how she'll get better. Total immersion. The transition is always hard no matter when you do it, but the earlier, the better." Mrs. Joyce gave her an understanding smile. "And remember, she won't be all alone. She'll have her sister. I will check on her and communicate with her teacher periodically."

This was no small consolation. Throughout everything, Jadelynn had been a godsend to both Christa and Elliana. Right after Christa's diagnosis, Elliana had wondered if she'd made a mistake adopting Jadelynn. Would she have enough time and energy for both, now that Christa demanded so much attention? Would Jadelynn resent her sister? Would she feel neglected, unloved—particularly since she was adopted?

But it turned out quite differently. Although Jadelynn and Christa fought and argued like sisters do, they were the best of friends. Despite being six months younger, Jadelynn took on almost a "big sister" role. A highly verbal extrovert, she often acted as Christa's translator to people outside the family while Christa's language skills were still developing.

In some ways, Elliana wondered if Christa's deafness might have actually helped Jadelynn deal with being adopted. Whereas Jadelynn might have felt like she didn't fit in because she looked different and wasn't biologically related, Christa's disability leveled the playing field and made her realize that everyone has their own unique challenges. And being Christa's spokesman gave her a sense of purpose and responsibility, an essential place in the family that she never would have had otherwise.

Elliana hoped that once again Jadelynn's high-spirited optimism and social skills would come to the fore and help ease Christa's transition. As it turned out, the school had a policy against putting siblings in the same class, but that didn't dampen Jadelynn's enthusiasm about Christa coming to her school.

"We can get lunch together and meet up between classes..." the ever-verbose Jadelynn rattled on happily.

✤ ✤ ✤

On the first day of school, the girls seemed excited, but Elliana was a bundle of nerves.

"Christa, here are extra batteries for you, just in case." Elliana inserted two packs of implant batteries in Christa's backpack's side pocket. Six little batteries the size of baby carrots were arranged like flower petals in each pack. They were small, but without them, Christa could be thrust back to the silent world with no warning.

Elliana kissed her on the forehead, but already Jadelynn was pulling Christa toward the door.

"Come ON!" she said. "We're gonna be late!"

All day Elliana was on pins and needles. *Oh please, let it go all right. Please.*

When the time to pick the girls up grew nearer, she could barely stand it any longer. She paced around the house; she sat down, then popped up again, only to wander around aimlessly again. Unable to wait any longer, she grabbed her keys and got in the car. She pulled up to the school fifteen minutes early. Each minute seemed to take an hour to pass.

Finally, the bell rang and the kids started pouring out of the building. Elliana spotted Christa in the line behind her new teacher. Her heart sank. While several of the children walked in pairs or groups, Christa was all by herself.

Elliana jumped out and joined the wave of parents

rushing toward the school to collect their kids. She made eye contact with Jadelynn, who was with her class, surrounded by a gaggle of young girls.

"I'm going to get Christa," she mouthed and Jadelynn nodded, turning back to her friends.

Christa's eyes lit up when she saw her mother.

Elliana bent down beside her. "So, how was your first day?" she chirped.

A cloud passed over her daughter's face. She shrugged.

"Remember, it takes a little while to make friends," Elliana said. "It didn't happen overnight at your other school either. You just have to give it time."

"Are we going to gymnastics class now?" Christa said, brightening. "We're doing back walkovers today!"

"Uh, sure," said Elliana. "As soon as we grab Jadelynn and get you changed."

On the drive home, Jadelynn regaled them with an animated description of her day, including everything she'd done in class and how she liked her new teachers and what all her friends had done over the summer.

Christa just stared out the window, silent.

❖ ❖ ❖

Over the next days and weeks, the discrepancy between Christa's demeanor around school compared to her bubbling excitement before and after gymnastics class only grew more obvious.

Elliana's worst fears were confirmed by her teacher, Ms. Canwright, at the first parent-teacher conference. Christa was doing okay academically, but socially, she seemed to be struggling. She was quiet and withdrawn, and didn't ever volunteer to answer questions, even though her papers showed she knew the answers.

"It's like she's afraid to be wrong," the teacher said.

"She is hard on herself," said Elliana, "but I don't know if it's that she's afraid of giving the wrong answer so much as she doesn't want to speak in front of the class. She's self-conscious about her speech."

Worst of all, she hadn't made any friends. Although she ate lunch with Jadelynn every day, that hadn't seemed to have widened her social circle. In fact, it might even have worked against her with her own classmates since she missed out on that prime bonding time with them.

Elliana's first instinct was to rip Christa out of school and take her right back to the auditory-oral school, where she was safe and supported and appreciated, and surrounded by friends. But she knew that she couldn't teach Christa to give up when the going gets hard. She had to help her stick it out. At least Christa still had gymnastics, which was a strong social network as well as a source of happiness, pride, and self-confidence.

School didn't get any better, and Christa seemed relieved when summer came and she could concentrate exclusively on gymnastics. To Elliana's disappointment, Christa didn't seem to make any new friends at the Academy like she had at the Y. Elliana had hoped the girls' shared passion would create a strong bond, but instead, there was a constant underlying competitiveness that made real friendship difficult.

Third grade got off to no better start than the year before. In fact, Christa's new teacher, Mr. Jenkins, seemed to have been sick the day they did sensitivity training. While Ms. Canwright had monitored Christa's social adjustment closely, Mr. Jenkins seemed to only care about Christa's performance on assignments and tests.

One day Elliana heard Christa crying in her bedroom.

"What's the matter, honey?" Elliana asked, alarmed. Tears were not uncommon for Jadelynn, who was emotive and tended toward the dramatic, but Christa hardly cried.

"It's nothing," Christa said, hurriedly wiping her tears.

Elliana sat on the bed. "C'mon, Christa. You can tell me."

"They said…" she started. Her lower lip began trembling and the tears came again. "They make fun of the way I talk. They say I sound like a retard!"

"Who did? Who said that?"

"The kids at school."

"Oh, honey!" Elliana pulled her daughter close and rocked her back and forth. Of course, she knew they were just children, but at that moment she could have clawed their eyes out. "Christa, you speak wonderfully!"

"No, I don't!"

"*Yes*, you do. You don't speak perfectly yet, but considering where you started, you are doing magnificently. And you are getting better all the time."

"I try *so* hard," Christa sniffed, her chin wobbling again.

"I know you do, sweetheart. You can't listen to them, okay? They don't know what they're talking about."

When Elliana told Mr. Jenkins about the incident, he only got defensive. "What do you expect me to do?" he asked. "I can't be everywhere. And kids need to learn to work out their own problems without overanxious adults" —he looked pointedly at Elliana—" swooping in and trying to 'fix' everything."

FLIPPING

Elliana gritted her teeth. After that, she was even more attentive to Christa's mood when she got home from school, trying to gauge her emotional temperature without bombarding her with questions. So it was a pleasant surprise when Christa came home from school one afternoon with a huge smile lighting up her face.

"What's got you grinning like the cat that swallowed the canary?" Elliana asked.

"There's a new boy in my class. He likes *Goosebumps*, just like me!"

"Oh, really?"

"Yeah!" said Jadelynn. "He ate lunch with us."

"Uh-huh," chimed in Christa. "And he doesn't care that I talk funny. He says I talk better than his dad!"

Elliana frowned, confused. "His dad? Is he deaf?"

The girls burst into peals of laughter, as if she'd said something extraordinarily funny.

"No!" said Jadelynn. "He's *Chinese*—like half of me!"

Elliana smothered a smile. "Oh, I see. *Chinese*."

"Yep," said Christa, picking up an apple from the bowl on the table and taking a big bite. "His name is Wynson and we're going to be *best friends.*"

Christa's love and passion for gymnastics grew with every new move she learned. She loved jumps, turns, and flipping in the air.

"Flipping in the air makes me feel free and alive," Christa told Jadelynn multiple times.

In the ENA Gymnastics and Dance Academy, she practiced from 4-8 p.m. on weekdays, and 8 a.m. to noon every Saturday. The session always started with warm-ups and conditioning: walking in a row, stretching, sit-ups, pull-ups, frog jumps, and then rotating through vault, uneven bars, the balance beam, and floor exercise. She reached Level 10 at fifth grade and won the all-around title!

But the 2008 Beijing Olympics was a game-changer for her. The family sat together for the opening ceremony. Elliana thought she might be able to use it as a teaching moment for Jadelynn to learn about Chinese culture. While she didn't want to force the issue, she wanted to give Jadelynn the opportunity to ask any questions she wanted to. But, instead, it was Christa who was glued to the screen.

"Look at this! Can you believe this?" Christa said breathlessly. The Chinese lion dance, the drums, the razor-sharp formations of people—the pageantry of the pre-game ceremony was nothing short of a religious experience for Christa.

Her favorite scene was the last one: the final ascent to the torch by Olympic gymnast Li Ning, who appeared to run through the air around the stadium. When Elliana turned off the set, Mitch and Jadelynn were already in bed and she was exhausted, but Christa was wide awake, humming like a live wire.

The rest of the games, Christa would come home from practice, scoop up a banana from the fruit bowl in the kitchen, and settle herself on the couch for the rest of the evening to keep up with the games. Even amidst the Chinese team controversy with He Kexin's fraudulent age, him being too young to compete, Christa was undeterred. The talent overwhelmed her and filled her with awe. Christa had witnessed talent at practice and high-pressure competitions, but these athletes were like human springs—petite, powerful springs. When she saw the lineup of the USA team in their shining red uniforms, eyes alight with euphoria and pride, Christa knew for a fact that she had caught the Olympic bug.

The teams are just machines, she thought. The gymnasts would swing on the uneven bars, faster and faster, all with a smile on their faces. (Coach Eugene said they would have to work on her presentation. "You're grimacing like you just smelled your underarms," he'd say.)

"How?" she muttered, watching the athletes. Their pivots bore a mechanical precision. Switching directions appeared to be nothing. And they landed after a few midair flips... like nothing. It seriously looked like nothing to them.

Christa, being familiar with the art, was incredulous. The gymnasts were beauty and power personified, perfectly blended together. They demonstrated utter control over everything. The roar of the crowds did not affect them. The pressure didn't appear to do anything but motivate them. They even defied the laws of physics.

When "The Star-Spangled Banner" swelled as Nastia Liukin and Shawn Johnson received their gold and silver medals, Christa looked as proud and reverent as if she were on the stand herself.

Christa finally saw an opportunity in her deafness. And it began with hard, hard labor at the gym. She asked for the poster of Shawn Johnson holding the Olympic gold medal as a Christmas gift, and when she received it, she posted it right next to her bed. Shawn's face was the first thing she greeted in the morning and the last thing she stared at before closing her eyes at night for years to come. Every time she looked at it, she imagined herself on the poster holding the gold medal.

This was the dream that sustained her.

FLIPPING

✢ ✢ ✢

It was early March. Elliana sipped tea, trying to calm her nerves. Christa had completed the compulsory step in the junior international elite process a couple of months earlier. Now, she was attempting to pass the optional skills test during a developmental training camp at the USA Gymnastics National Team Training Center at Texas.

It was a long two days. Finally, the phone rang.

"She finished at 53.10 all around: 13.25 for vault, 12.35 for uneven bars, 14.0 for balance beam, and 13.5 for floor exercise. She made it!" Coach Eugene could not conceal his excitement.

A few minutes later, "Mom, I passed it." A text from Christa. She had qualified as a junior international elite gymnast. A step closer to her dream.

✢ ✢ ✢

I need more complex skills and routines. I need to perform perfectly!

"Christa, I know what you are thinking. You want more difficult skills and connections. We will work on it. Remember, one move at a time. Not so rushed," Coach Eugene said.

"I want to be in the USA Gymnastics National Championships! I want to be on the junior national team! I want to be in the International Elites!" Christa said with resolve. She could hardly catch her breath. She had the route mapped out. She knew exactly what she aimed for.

Part Three

The Kids

Chapter 7

Christa's concentration was total. Nothing existed except her and the beam. The smooth wood was worn down by years of leaps, prances, backbends, and Christa loved its familiarity; it was an extension of her. On the beam, she was powerful, focused, completely in flow.

The trick was keeping militaristic control over both mind and body. There was no room for thinking about anything except the next move—not whatever had happened in school that day or what anyone watching thought about her technique, or even how she could have done better on her less than perfect flying flairs a few seconds ago. Fear, pain, regret, self-consciousness—all had to be abolished. Only the present moment mattered.

Christa stood still, preparing for her dismount: a cartwheel going into a stretched-back salto with a double twist. Every single fiber of her body was alive. She clenched her powerhouse muscles and rose on the balls of her feet before exploding forward. The rush, the exhilaration of flying through the air—it was over in a split second. She'd stuck the landing, but just barely.

Sloppy, she berated herself. She needed to be like a knife, piercing the ground in a focused landing. *It's got to be perfect.*

Suddenly a hand on her shoulder nearly made her jump out of her skin. She spun around.

"Oh, Wynson!" she said. "You just about gave me a heart attack. Hold on a sec. Lemme get my ears on." She walked over to her gym bag and got out the behind-the-ear processor for her cochlear implant. Christa switched on the processor, and the outside world came back online.

Wynson and Jadelynn were frequent visitors of the gym. The receptionist was familiar with them and felt comfortable allowing them to walk in the training area freely.

"Sorry, guys," she said. "Is it already eight? I lost track of time."

"No problem," Wynson replied. "We're not in any hurry. At least Jadelynn isn't. She's been having a grand old time stripping me of every remaining ounce of manhood that I managed to leave the court with."

"Can I help it if you lost?" Jadelynn teased. "What did you want me to do, go easy on you?"

"It wasn't an even match," he insisted. "My shoulder's still not a hundred percent after I pulled it in practice last week." He rubbed his shoulder for effect.

"It wasn't your shoulder; it's your lousy backhand. Always has been."

"Awww, Wynson, did Jadelynn beat you again?" Christa said in mock sympathy.

"Again? What *again*? That other time was a travesty of justice! The official must have been blind—or else he was just too busy looking at Jadelynn's skimpy little skirt to notice where the ball was." He was joking, but it was true that Jadelynn's long legs and exotic beauty turned heads wherever

128

she went. And the precocious sixteen-year-old was well aware of the effect she had on the males of the species.

Jadelynn batted her eyes innocently. "Can I help it if tennis skirts are so short?"

"And men are such Neanderthals?" chimed in Christa.

"Oh, right," said Wynson, doing an impressive imitation of a grunting, knuckle-scraping, ogling hominid. The girls dissolved in laughter.

"So, Christa, are you coming out tonight?" asked Jadelynn. "Meredith's parents are out of town, so she's having a party."

"I don't think so," said Christa. "I've got to get up early."

"Oh, c'mon. It's just one night. Live a little!"

"I've got World in less than a month," Christa insisted.

Jadelynn appealed to Wynson. "Will you tell my sister she needs to lighten up? One night out isn't going to kill her."

"Well, I guess if I was going to do something to jeopardize a world championship, it probably wouldn't be one of Michelle Dupree's famous drunk fests," he said.

Christa shot him a grateful look.

"Fine. Be a homebody," Jadelynn said. Then she grabbed Christa's gym bag and took off for the door. "Race ya to the car!" she called over her shoulder.

Wynson and Christa ran out to the parking lot to find Jadelynn nonchalantly leaning up against Wynson's cherry-red Mercedes. It had been a gift from his parents on his sixteenth birthday. He would have preferred something less showy—a Honda or maybe a Prius—but he kept his reservations to himself because the only thing more obnoxious than having a flashy, overpriced car was complaining about it.

"Took you long enough," she said with a wink, tossing Christa's bag to her. "I call shotgun."

They stopped at the drive-thru for milkshakes, and Jadelynn treated Wynson and Christa to a hysterical blow-by-blow account of her day, including a spot-on impression of their vice principal, who spoke with an unfortunate lisp.

"Mith McMerith?" she mimicked, peering down her nose. "Why aren't you in clath, Mith McMerith? Do you have a path? A path, Mith McMerith. A path for clath?"

"Stop!" cried Christa, laughing so hard, tears were running down her cheeks. "You're going to give me the hiccups!"

"The hiccups?" scoffed Jadelynn. "Oh, no, my dear. I won't be happy until at least one of you is squirting milkshake out their nose."

"I nominate Christa," said Wynson. "You wouldn't want me to wreck, would you?"

"Now that you mention it," said Jadelynn, "a wrecked car *would* be a feather in my cap!"

Wynson suddenly jerked the wheel and tapped the brakes, causing both girls to shriek in surprise. "Sorry," he said. "Invisible squirrel."

This was how it always was with them. There was a chemistry, a special energy when they were together. Somehow, they just fit.

Wynson and Christa had clicked from day one. Quiet, reserved, and serious, he and Christa were cut from the same cloth, like twins separated at birth. Jadelynn, on the other hand, couldn't have been more different. Lighthearted and always laughing, she was the yin to their yang, the salt to their starch. Even though Jadelynn was a social butterfly with a million friends, there was never any question that Wynson and Christa were her best buds.

They were the Three Amigos.

As he pulled into the McMeris' driveway and dropped the girls off, Wynson watched them disappear into the house.

What would happen if she knew how I really felt? he wondered. He had never had a hint that she returned his feelings, and the three-way friendship was too important to him to jeopardize.

At least I can be close to her, even if it is just as friends...

When he arrived at his house, Wynson parked in the four-car garage and went in the side door, which he always preferred to the imposing front entrance. Even though they had lived there for nearly two years, it still didn't feel like home to Wynson. It was too big, too formal. And worst of all, he couldn't get over the feeling it had been bought with blood money during the financial crisis of 2008. For many, this was a devastating period; for JonSun, it provided the window of golden opportunity for which he had hoped for many years.

In early 2006, JonSun foresaw the burst of housing bubbles.

No doc, no income, no credit check—easy home loans are ticking bombs. The party has to be over soon.

As JonSun refrained from over-aggressively flipping properties, he decided to put his twenty-unit shopping center in Anaheim up for sale. With the renovation, careful landscaping, and repaved parking lot, the strip mall's business had grown rapidly in the few years since they bought it. The only concern JonSun had was that it had no major anchor store—just a Mexican restaurant, a Japanese restaurant, a flower shop, a coin laundry, and some mom-and-pop stores. Still, the strip mall was sold in a month to a group of investors. JonSun realized later that some of them took a second or third mortgage on their primary homes as down payment for the purchase.

JonSun used the proceeds of the shopping mall to buy a rundown medical plaza and a chunk of a mobile home park as part of his income properties portfolio. He tapered off the house-flipping activities and focused on strengthening his income properties and accumulating cash.

He did just that, sat on the cash, and waited for the market to hit bottom.

"Dad, don't you feel guilty profiting off other people's misery?" Wynson had asked one day as his father pored over the listings of foreclosed bank-owned properties and short-sale houses.

"No, of course not," JonSun said, surprised. "Why should I? I am helping the recovery of the economy. Banks should thank me for reducing their toxic inventory. Government should be delighted that I am paying the taxes."

Wynson couldn't argue with his father's logic, but something about it still didn't sit right with him. After winding his way through the house, Wynson finally found his parents sitting on the porch, enjoying the final days of the palatial garden that required a virtual fleet of workers to keep trimmed and manicured.

"Would you like some tea?" his mother asked.

"No, I'm fine. I was wondering, could we have Jadelynn over for dinner sometime? We have a cultural heritage project, and she wants to learn more about Taiwanese culture."

"I would love that!" SuAnn said excitedly. "You hardly have any of your friends over. I could make a traditional dinner and we could get out our photo albums and some of our things from Taiwan. And your father could show her his art collection... wouldn't that be fun, honey?" She looked at her husband eagerly.

"And what about you, son?" asked JonSun. "What will your project be on?"

Wynson shrugged noncommittally. "I haven't decided yet." In truth, he already knew—he was going to do an oral history of his family's immigration—but these days everything his father asked somehow felt like an invasion of privacy. Wynson examined even the most innocuous-seeming questions for possible ulterior motives.

JonSun let the matter drop. "Son, would you like to go to the attorney's office with me next Monday? I have an appointment with LaShawn. I've checked your school calendar. You have no class on that day."

"Why?" Wynson asked suspiciously. He was sure his father didn't just want the pleasure of his company.

LaShawn Goldbern had been Tang's real estate attorney for years. He was six-foot-four and African-American. In his youth, he had been accepted to Stanford with a basketball scholarship, an NBA hopeful. A near-death automobile accident right before his college graduation dashed his dreams of becoming a professional basketball player. After the tragedy, he went to Yale Law School and specialized in real estate law. His motto was "He who limps is still walking."

When Wynson first met Mr. Goldbern, he had immediately looked up to the tall, suave man with a million-dollar smile and the brains to match. Since then, JonSun had taken him along to some of his business meetings with his attorney in the thinly disguised hope that Wynson would be inspired to consider law as a profession.

"I've decided on a condominium conversion to subdivide the twenty-four-unit building we just bought in South Orange County, and I need LaShawn to prepare all the legal paperwork," his father said. "I thought you could ask him about your college plans."

Wynson was in the process of taking the SATs and ACTs and preparing for college applications. Two particular schools he had in mind. There was UC Berkeley, where he would attend for his undergraduate degree; Columbia offered an accelerated JD program, where he'd receive his undergraduate degree along with a JD in just six years.

Even though he was predisposed to object to any suggestion his father made, Wynson realized he actually wouldn't mind getting Mr. Goldbern's take on the matter. He couldn't think of a better advisor. Unlike his father, the lawyer gave him the facts without trying to make his decision for him. So, he accompanied his father to the office.

✤ ✤ ✤

"Hey! What up, my friend?" Mr. Goldbern stood up and walked over to greet them. His gigantic proportions dwarfed Wynson's slim five-eleven frame.

"Doing all right," Wynson said, giving him a fist bump.

"All right? He's Student Council president, newspaper editor, and straight A's!" JonSun boasted.

"I just write for the paper," Wynson corrected. "I'm not the editor." His father's bragging made him feel like a prize cow. "Um, real quick. Is it okay if I take a couple minutes of your time? I'd like to ask your opinion on something."

"Sure. What's happening? You in trouble with the law?" Goldbern joked.

"Well, it's about school." Wynson explained his indecision about UC Berkeley versus the accelerated JD program at Columbia University.

After chatting for a while, Mr. Goldbern's advice to Wynson was: "If you want to take time to evaluate your true passion, it would be a good idea to go through four years of your undergrad and explore all options before committing to a professional school. But, if you are a hundred percent sure that you want to be in law—no question—the accelerated JD program makes sense because it'll save you time."

Definitely something to think about, Wynson thought. "Thanks for the advice." He smiled with gratitude. Saving time…well, that sounded good. Then he could get out into the world and start dominating the law profession. That is, if he could commit.

❖ ❖ ❖

Christa paced around her room. Nine o'clock on a Friday night and she was home alone. As usual. She wondered if should she have gone out with Jadelynn. She was a teenager, after all. Shouldn't she *want* to be going out to parties?

But it wasn't as if she had never been to one before. And

they were never as much fun as they were supposed to be. She knew how it would go: she'd spend the whole night feeling awkward and self-conscious, following Jadelynn around like a little puppy and counting the minutes until they could leave.

Part of it was the drinking. Yes, it was illegal to have alcohol at their age, but they did it anyway in private. Christa never drank because she was afraid the hangover would ruin her workouts the next day, and she was too careful with what she put in her body to knowingly poison herself. But she found that without the social lubricant of alcohol, the stories and jokes that everyone else seemed to find hysterical were completely lost on her. Plus, not drinking made people think she was a prissy goody-two-shoes.

And tonight would be even worse than usual since Jadelynn wouldn't be around to babysit her all night because she had a new friend, Jackson, that she'd want to hang out with.

Christa had never had a boyfriend. In fact, she'd never even been kissed, except for one horrible sloppy one by Martin Brubaker at an end-of-school dance back in middle school that she later found he'd done on a dare. At only four-feet ten, Christa still had a preadolescent body, perfect for gymnastics, but not exactly what hormonal teenage boys were looking for.

It doesn't matter, I have my priority, she told herself. She didn't have time to date anyway.

She looked around the room at all the medals and trophies, and the poster of Shawn Johnson on the podium. *That* was what it was all about.

Olympic gold.

Christa could still remember how she felt watching her

first Olympics. The talent overwhelmed her. The gymnasts' strength, agility, flexibility, and balance seemed superhuman. The courage to perform complicated tricks and compete under intense pressure required ultimate focus. The proper body alignment, the swift repulsion, the flips and twists, the split second of release and re-grasp, the leaps, turns, series of tumbling moves, and rapid change of directions in a graceful movement were the result of hours and hours of painstaking practice. The gymnasts were the beauty and power artistically blended together.

That was who she wanted to be.

The training regimen for an Olympic hopeful was brutal. Christa worked out at home for an hour before school, then went to the gym for a four-hour practice every day after school. Weekends meant more practice as well as competitions. Christa couldn't remember the last time she went shopping, enjoyed the luxury of reading a book, or took a day off. Her entire life revolved around gymnastics.

And it wasn't just Christa's life; her passion had become a family affair. Her mother had become so knowledgeable about the sport, she could evaluate and advise Christa on her technique almost as well as Coach Eugene. Christa's father took on extra work to pay for her training, and he always helped choose the music for her floor routines. Moreover, Jadelynn was Christa's personal stylist and biggest cheerleader.

Christa knew that every win was as much a win for her family as for her. If she had to give up parties, boyfriends, a "regular" teenage life, it was a small price to pay.

Nothing's going to keep me down. Nothing.

❖ ❖ ❖

The next week, Jadelynn came for dinner at the Tangs'.

"I can't believe this is the first time I've been to your house since you moved here," she said when Wynson opened the door.

He shrugged. His traditional parents didn't understand the concept of male-female friendships and would under no circumstances allow Wynson to be unsupervised with a girl. It was easier to just hang out elsewhere.

Jadelynn ran her hand along the large, deep burgundy, lacquered armoire cabinet in the foyer. "It's gorgeous!" she said, her eyes going to the dramatic dragon painting on the opposite wall.

Wynson shrugged. "Qing dynasty."

"How long ago was that?"

"Early 1800s. My dad is a *collector,* so nearly everything in the house is antique. We'll get him to give you the grand tour after dinner. He enjoys boring the pants off guests, telling them where each piece is from, its history, the construction techniques, how much he paid for it... Normally I wouldn't subject you to it, but it might help with your project."

"Dinner's ready," his mom called.

The smell of ginger sesame oil mixed with fresh green onion greeted them before they entered the dining room. The table was set with beautiful china hand-painted with delicate blue designs. His father was already seated at the head of the long table.

"It smells wonderful, Mrs. Tang," said Jadelynn. "What is it?"

"Stir-fried beef minced with celery and string beans in oyster sauce, Kung Pao shrimp, and steamed fish with ginger and garlic. I hope you like it."

"My parents have been in the States for nearly two

decades, but their accent remained," Wynson said apologetically.

"Oh, Wynson, your parents speak English beautifully," Jadelynn said, then turned to his parents. "The only time we have Chinese is takeout," she confessed.

Wynson's dad snorted derisively. "That, Americanized. This, the real thing!" He gazed at his wife proudly. "My wife is best cook in Taipei."

"Oh, is that where you're from? I thought you were from Taiwan."

Wynson saw his father shoot his mother a look.

"Taipei is *in* Taiwan," Wynson hurried to explain. "Taiwan is the whole island and Taipei is its capital. But don't worry; lots of people don't know that."

"Oh," said Jadelynn easily. "I guess that's one of the things I'll need to research!"

Wynson realized that he needn't have tried to spare her feelings. While he and Christa would have been mortified if they hadn't known such a basic fact, it didn't faze Jadelynn at all.

"My birth mom is from Taiwan," she continued. "I'd like to go there someday."

Wynson was surprised. He'd heard the story about Jadelynn's adoption way back when they first met, but since then he'd never heard her talking about her birth mom or wanting to visit Taiwan. He asked her about it when he was driving her home after his father finally wrapped up his interminable tour of the estate.

"So, Jade. You mentioned your birth mom tonight. You never talk about her. Do you ever think about getting in touch with her?"

"Oh, no, nothing like that," she said quickly. Wynson

thought a little too quickly.

"Really? C'mon, you haven't even thought about it? Why not?"

Jadelynn shrugged. "I love my parents now. I don't feel the need to look for her; that may complicate the situation. Besides, she knows how to get in touch with Mom. We still live at the same house she lived in when she was their exchange student! If she wanted to be in contact, she would be."

Wynson weighed this. "Maybe…" he said. "But maybe not. Maybe she doesn't want to intrude, and she's waiting for you to reach out if *you* want to."

Jadelynn paused. "I guess it's *possible*…"

"I bet she would love to know how you're doing. It must be horrible not knowing. Can you imagine what that would be like for her? I mean, you *know* she's a good person. Giving you up wasn't something she wanted to do; she had to."

"I know. You're right. She probably does wonder about me. But I don't want to mess up her life. The whole reason she gave me up was because she didn't want her family to know… What if I write and they find out? What if she's married and has other kids and *they* find out?"

Wynson considered this. "Well, what if you wrote sort of in code? Your mom was her host mother, right? So would it be so strange if you were to get in touch with her?" He thought for a moment. "You could use this project as an excuse. Say that you're doing a project on Taiwan and you knew she was a friend of your mom's so you're writing to learn about what life there is like… That way if someone found the letter, it wouldn't matter."

A slow smile spread across Jadelynn's face. "You know, that isn't such a bad idea! I could write it so *she* knows that I know, but no one else reading it would catch on. It'd be like James Bond!" Wynson started humming the *Mission Impossible* theme song.

Jadelynn joined in and soon they were belting it out at the top of their lungs. When they finished, Wynson grew serious.

"I think you should do it, Jade."

"Really?" she said. "I thought of it once in a while, but I didn't want to hurt my parents' feelings. And…I guess I was scared she wouldn't want me…" Her voice caught. She was crying!

Wynson was taken aback. Jadelynn was always happy and bubbly, the life of the party. He'd never seen her nervous or insecure. *This must go deep,* he thought. He pulled the car over to the side of the road.

"Shoot, Jadelynn. I'm sorry. I didn't mean to upset you."

"No, it's okay. It's not your fault."

"Here, give me a hug," he said. He held her close for a long moment. When they drew apart, he looked her straight in the eye. "She might not write you back. That's a possibility you have to be prepared for. But if she doesn't, that's totally on her. It's got *nothing* to do with you. She doesn't even know you, so how could it? Promise me, you'll remember that, okay?"

Jadelynn sniffled. "Okay, promise."

"Good. If she doesn't want to know you, believe me, it's her loss."

She gave him a luminous smile—the smile that had captured so many boys' hearts.

"Thanks. You're a great friend."

✤ ✤ ✤

Christa checked in by the entrance and received her number. She looked around, overwhelmed by the sheer size of the stadium, the din of the crowd, the enormity of just being there.

It was the World Championship.

I wish Jadelynn was here. No matter how nervous Christa got, her sister could always make her laugh and calm her nerves. But they couldn't afford for the whole family to go, so only her mother was there. They were so grateful that the local Lion Clubs and a couple of private business entities had sponsored the entire trip.

Jadelynn had Skyped her the night before to give her a pep talk, but it wasn't the same as having her there in person.

"Okay, I'm going to go up and find my seat," her mom said. "But I'll be watching you the whole time. If you need me, just give me the signal and I will try to get to you. Remember the signal?"

"Yes, Mom." Christa touched her chin with two fingers on her right hand.

"That's it, sweetheart."

Christa nodded.

"Okay. Now, don't you worry. You're going to do *great*," her mother said, giving her a hug. "Remember, you're superhuman, right?" She looked right into her eyes.

That had been their little joke from when Christa was little and the other kids would tease her about her processor. Her mother always said it made her special, like a superpower.

That was her, the bionic girl.

Her mom shifted her gaze and smiled. Here came Coach Eugene. Seeing them, his weathered face broke into a smile. Her mother left to find her seat.

"How are you doing?" he asked. It was a real question. At this level, managing your emotions was every bit as important as mastering the physical skills.

"Um, I'm a little shaky..." she admitted.

Coach Eugene gripped her by the shoulders and brought her attention to his face. "Don't worry about them," he said. "You just concentrate on what you're here for. Close your eyes, take a deep breath, and center yourself."

Christa did as she was told.

"Now visualize your routine. You've got the bars first. Play the movie." As part of her training, Coach Eugene had filmed Christa's routines so she could see her errors and weaknesses. Then he'd taken her best performances—the near-flawless ones—and had her watch them over and over again, etching them into her brain. He claimed visualization was just as effective as actually executing a perfect routine. Your brain couldn't tell the difference.

Christa went through the swings and twists, the kips and casts, imagining it all so meticulously that she could feel the chalk in her hands and the rush of air as she circled the bar. Finally, she envisioned her dismount—a double twisting double back called the Fabrichnova. She felt her feet hit the mat solidly without a step or even a wobble. Arms above her head, she beamed victoriously at the cheering crowd. She opened her eyes and nodded at Coach Eugene. Her head was back in the game.

She began stretching and warming up her muscles. She chalked her hands. Finally, when it was nearly time for her to compete, she went over to her gym bag and removed her processor. That was her secret weapon. By simply taking off the processor, she retreated to the world of silence once again. In practice, but particularly in competitions, it eliminated distracting background noise and improved her concentration and performance.

Coach Eugene gave her a hand signal when her name was called. Christa advanced to the bars. From that point on, time passed in a blur. Christa was completely in the zone. She ignored the crowds; she didn't watch the other gymnasts; she concentrated only on her own performance. When she made a mistake or misstep, she noted it, filed it away to be processed later, and immediately moved on. Only the present mattered.

Be a machine.

She advanced to the balance beam; her front walkover, double turn in split, and two flip-flops to a double pike dismount won her much applause. She performed admirably on the floor exercise; the audience clapped with the music. Her Arabian double front and double back with double twist, connected with graceful dance moves in between, won her high marks. Her moves were completely in sync with the music; everyone forgot she could not hear it at all.

At last, she nailed her best event, the vault, scoring a 15.50 to place second.

Christa qualified for the all-around competition. When the final results came in, she was second overall. Her mother was ecstatic.

"I can't believe it!" she shouted.

"My baby is second in THE WORLD!" She high-fived her daughter and did a goofy victory dance.

Jadelynn was equally enthusiastic on Skype. She greeted Christa with a huge congratulations banner and a cake when she got home. It had a "Sweet 16" candle surrounded by four little marzipan gymnasts on each of the apparatus.

"Way to go, sis!" she exclaimed.

Christa tried to look excited for the sake of her family. She knew it was no small accomplishment and she should be proud of herself.

But second wasn't a victory when you were dreaming of gold in the Olympics.

⁘ ⁘ ⁘

"C'mon, Christa!" Jadelynn insisted. "It'll be fun! Everyone will be there." The bonfire on the beach was a tradition for the teenagers on Halloween night.

Turning back to the mirror, Jadelynn rubbed her thumb in black face paint and colored in her nose. She perused the bathroom drawers until she found her mother's lip brush, and then used it to draw three whiskers on each of her cheeks. With that, she admired herself in the mirror, straightening her black ears.

"I don't know..." said Christa doubtfully. It would be loud and dark to boot, so she wouldn't even be able to lip read. It sounded like a long night of feeling frustrated and left out. There was nothing like a big crowd to make you feel alone.

The loneliest loneliness is feeling alone in a big crowd.

"Girls!" their father called from hallway. "Wynson's here!"

Jadelynn put her finger to her mouth and waited for Wynson to come up. "Grr!" she cried, jumping out of the bathroom with a growl. Wynson, decked out in a top hat and tails, pretended to jump in fear.

"You're a scary cat, Jade," he said.

"I'm not a cat. I'm a panther." She playfully pawed the air.

"Oh, sorry. You guys ready to go?"

"We've got to get *her* ready," Jadelynn said, pointing to Christa.

"I don't have anything to wear," Christa insisted. "You just go on without me."

"Nonsense! Come with me!" commanded Jadelynn, heading for her room. Ever the clothes hound and fashionista, she scoffed at people who thought they were being fashionable when they wore things they got at the mall. To Jadelynn, having a sense of style meant being different, not just following the crowd. She got many of her inimitable one-of-a-kind outfits from vintage stores or even Savers.

"Here," she said, pulling out a beaded dress from the closet. "We'll smooth out your hair and put a headband around your forehead and ta-da! You're a flapper!"

Christa still looked uncertain.

"If you're a flapper, we can go as a couple," said Wynson, picking up on the real reason behind Christa's hesitation. "This suit could be from the twenties easy."

"Oh, all right," she agreed, reluctantly. "If you *insist*."

"We do!"

Jadelynn soon had Christa ready to go and they piled into Wynson's car. Soon they pulled into the parking lot alongside another couple of cars full of kids. They started walking down to the beach.

Wynson noticed that for some reason, Christa seemed to move with two left feet. She stumbled not once, but twice within five minutes. The next thing he knew, she was sprawled out on the ground.

"Sorry," she mumbled.

"No worries," Wynson said, helping her up. "Are you okay, though?"

"Yes." Christa shifted uncomfortably. "Go ahead, keep up with the others." Jadelynn had already disappeared up ahead with some of her friends.

"Are you kidding? What kind of gentleman leaves his lady in the lurch?"

Christa rolled her eyes. She got up and they started walking again. Christa moved slowly, picking her way carefully. Suddenly, she fell again.

"What's going on? Are you okay?" Wynson asked.

"I'm *fine*," she said emphatically.

"You're not fine," he said. Her tights were ripped at the knees, and both kneecaps were scraped and bleeding. "I'm taking you home."

"No way! We're almost there. I'll be fine."

"Look, you didn't even want to come. Let's just go back to your house and get you cleaned up and we'll watch *Night of the Living Dead*. They're having a zombie marathon tonight."

"I don't want you to miss out on the party."

"Oh, c'mon. You know I like parties about as much as you do. And besides, do you know how hot this suit is? I didn't even think about the fact we'd be at a *bonfire*. I'm going to roast!"

"Fine," she reluctantly acquiesced.

"Great. You stay here and I'll go tell Jadelynn what happened and make sure she's got someone to drive her home."

✤ ✤ ✤

Christa's parents greeted them at the door when they heard Wynson's car pull up.

"What happened? You okay?" her dad said when he saw Wynson supporting Christa up the walkway.

"Christa had a few falls," Wynson began. Christa shot him a dangerous look.

"A few?" her mother asked. She eyed Christa's body from top to bottom, stopping at the knees and then rapidly looking for a cause. "What is it? The shoes?"

"I'm wearing flats," Christa said. Her face reflected slight exasperation. "I'm really fine."

"Well, why did you keep falling?"

"I don't know why. It was really dark, and I couldn't see well."

"When did she last have an eye exam?" her father asked her mom.

"Less than a year ago. Dr. Tanmura said her eyes were fine, no problems at all. I could make an appointment for tomorrow?"

"It was dark," Christa repeated, but her mother's mind was made up. She would be making an appointment first thing in the morning. In the meantime, she went for some first aid for Christa's shredded knees. Within seconds she had wet a cotton ball with hydrogen peroxide and dabbed it on the wounds. Christa squeezed her eyes tight and endured the anxious ministrations without complaint.

"You didn't have to tell them I fell *twice*," Christa hissed when they were finally alone in the TV room.

"Why shouldn't I? Has this happened before?"

Christa stared at the television as if she hadn't heard him.

Wynson allowed his eyes to be drawn to the movie, but the nervous knot forming in his stomach had nothing to do with the monsters on the screen.

Chapter 8

H ey, Christa, congratulations! I saw your pictures and articles on your gymnastics achievements in the paper." Dr. Tanmura, a kind-faced Japanese optometrist in his forties, beamed when he saw his patient. He had been Christa and Jadelynn's eye doctor since they were in preschool and always seemed to remember the happenings in their lives—and inquired about them at each visit.

"Thank you," Christa replied with a small smile.

"Your parents must be very proud of you." He spoke in a normal voice but faced her squarely to make sure she heard him well. His face visibly shifted from pride to concern as he spotted the large square Band-Aids on her knees. "Oh, what happened? From practice?"

"She fell while walking down to the beach, multiple times," her mother cut in. "She said she couldn't see because everything was too dark."

So began the interrogation. Dr. Tanmura asked more questions and typed the detailed history in his computer, then proceeded with the routine exam.

"Okay, Christa. I'm going to check your visual field, I mean the peripheral vision, and then I'll put drops in your eyes for the dilated fundus exam. Your eyes will be dilated for about four to six hours."

"You'll have to miss practice today," her mother added gently.

Christa sighed. Her mother knew she hated missing gymnastics practice. *At least the visual field test is cool*, Christa thought. *Like a computer game*. But not the dilation.

She sat in the reception area waiting for the eyedrops to take effect, not knowing what to say to her mother. She pulled her cell phone out, tweeted that she hated eye dilations, and within minutes, everything on her phone screen became a blur. With a big sigh, she tucked her cell phone back into her jean hip pocket. In few seconds, she felt the vibrations on her hip. *Someone must've replied or re-tweeted me*. She did not bother to check.

Even though she knew it was part of the routine, there was something about losing her precious eyesight that bothered her, even if only briefly. It was a double handicap. She imagined what it would be like to be both deaf and blind like her mother's hero, Helen Keller. *She must have felt so isolated. Thank goodness I've only got to deal with it temporarily. A couple of hours is bad enough.*

Later, Dr. Tanmura intently studied the digital retinal photos of Christa's eyes on the monitor screen. He clicked on the button on the sidebar to pull out the photos from three years ago, which he had taken as a baseline.

"Something wrong?" Christa's mother quickly asked.

"The fundus, I mean the background of Christa's eyes, has changed. These unusual pigment deposits weren't there before." Dr. Tanmura pointed to an area located in the large, veiny orb on the screen. He continued cautiously. "This could explain the cause of her many falls the other night."

Turning to face Christa, he asked, "How long have you noticed that you don't see well at night?"

"For a while." Christa shifted uncomfortably as she tried to think back. "I don't know."

"I'm going to refer you to the Retinal Institute of Los Angeles."

Christa stared blankly as the doctor wrote the ominous words on the referral form:

Patient experienced night blindness.

Significant clinical findings: Visual field restriction (see attached)

Bone spicule pigmentation at mid-peripheral fundus (digital retinal photo, will forward)

Please perform:
   -ERG (Electroretinogram)
   -OCT (Optical Coherence Tomography)
   -FA (Fluorescein Angiogram)

She didn't like the sound of the tests, but before she could think to ask any questions, Dr. Tanmura added, "I also recommend a blood test at the South Bay Genetic Lab. I want to look into a condition called Usher syndrome. The majority of patients with Usher syndrome have difficulties with balance. However, Christa has no problem with that—clearly, as she's an accomplished gymnast—so it's an unlikely scenario. But we should rule it out." Dr. Tanmura spoke gently, but Christa felt the hair rise defensively along her neck.

It's just to eliminate the possibility, she told herself as he led them toward the front desk. *I'm a gymnast. I don't have balance problems. I can't have whatever it is he's checking for.*

❖ ❖ ❖

Dr. Larmount, the chief of ophthalmology, congratulated Christa on her achievements. "I saw your article in *The LA Times*," he said. "Great meeting you in person."

Christa nodded, just wanting him to skip the pleasantries and get down to business. She was supposed to get her final diagnosis today.

As Dr. Larmount sat down, he extracted the referral form from Dr. Tanmura and explained the tests. After going over all the results, he summarized the findings methodically as he undoubtedly had done many, many times before.

"What this all means," he faced Christa and her mother squarely and said, "is that Christa has a condition called *retinitis pigmentosa*. The lab faxed over the genetic report as we requested earlier today. The genetic test confirms that Christa has a condition called Usher syndrome. This would cause a person to become deaf and lose their eyesight later on."

Christa couldn't believe the matter-of-fact tone he used to deliver the diagnosis to them. Surely he couldn't have just said what she thought he said. She was going to lose her eyesight too?

Christa tried to pay attention, but she had a hard time focusing on what the doctor was saying. She saw his lips moving and heard his voice through the implant, but she just caught bits and pieces before her mind would flit away again.

"Usher syndrome is the result of a genetic mutation and the leading cause of deafness and blindness."

"Retinal cells degenerate in the eye. The inner ear is

dysfunctional."

"Her field of view will be gradually constricted as tunnel vision."

"There is no guaranteed treatment at this time, although there are plenty of research studies going on…"

Christa was too stunned to speak, but her mother was full of questions. "I Googled Usher syndrome as soon as Dr. Tanmura mentioned it," she said. "It seems unpredictable, that even the most experienced and knowledgeable professionals wouldn't be able to say how fast or how badly the disease would progress. Is that true?"

"I'm afraid so. Each case is unique. Some people lose their sight very rapidly; others have a very slow progression."

Blind! Christa wanted to run out of the room and away from the awful words bombarding her. Pent-up rage and wild fear crushed her.

This is so unfair! she mentally screamed. *Wasn't it enough that I have to be deaf? Now I'm going to be blind too? Why? Why me? What did I do wrong?*

Thoughts flooded her mind, each more awful than the last. What would this mean for her gymnastics? Would she still be able to compete for the Olympics? Would she lose her independence? How would she communicate? Would she be alone the rest of her life? Even Helen Keller had never gotten married, despite all her fame and accomplishments. Who would want to be with someone who was both deaf *and* blind?

✢ ✢ ✢

Elliana led the family to say grace as usual. She asked God to give the family strength, guidance, and wisdom through all the trials. The dinner was quiet, heavy with anticipation of the difficult conversation to come. Christa moved her food around on her plate, feeling the weight of everyone's eyes on her.

Her father finally broke the ice. "Christa, how do you feel about Dr. Larmount's diagnosis? About your eyes?"

"I don't know," Christa said.

"What do you mean, you don't know?" he asked, not harshly.

"I see fine during the daytime now, and I don't want to think about it." Christa pushed the peas around her plate and didn't look up so she couldn't see what her parents had to say. But when she did look up, her mother spoke the words she'd been afraid of hearing.

"Dad and I think you should stop gymnastics."

Christa blinked at the news. It took a few seconds before she responded in a deadly voice. "Kill me first if you want me to stop gymnastics." She could see how much her words hurt her mother, but she didn't care.

"We know how much gymnastics means to you," her mother said. "We just worry about your safety."

"That's right," her father said. "Your safety is more important than anything else. Gymnastics is a very dangerous sport, Christa. You've already had one injury. If you have problems with your eyesight, it will make it all the more likely you'll be hurt again—possibly worse."

Christa was furious. "I lost my hearing and I'm losing my sight. I'm not losing gymnastics too!" She shoved her chair away from the table and ran to her room, collapsing on the bed in tears.

Her parents had always told her she could do anything she set her mind to, not to let anything or anyone stand in her way. And now they wanted her to *quit*? She felt like the rug had been pulled out from under her.

A few minutes later, a tentative knock came at her bedroom door.

"Can I come in?" Jadelynn called.

"Yeah," said Christa, although all she really wanted was to be left alone to wallow in self-pity.

Jadelynn opened the door and sat down at the end of Christa's bed. She was uncharacteristically somber.

"You know, this really sucks," she said.

"Y'think?" Christa said into the pillow.

"Yeah, I do. But I also think you're overlooking the upside."

Christa rolled over and eyed her sister skeptically. Jadelynn had a mischievous gleam in her eye. "Okay. You got me. The upside?"

"A dog. We can finally get a dog! I can even help you train it."

That is Jadelynn for you, Christa thought to herself. *Ever the optimist.* Christa wasn't nearly as excited as she knew Jadelynn wanted her to be—in fact, the idea of a guide dog made the prospect of going blind all the more horrifyingly real—but her sister was trying so hard to make her feel better. They all were.

"Do you really think Dad would let us? He's always said no before..." said Christa, faking an interest she didn't feel.

Jadelynn looked at her like she'd grown horns. "Are you *kidding*? You think he'd be able to say no to *anything* you want now? He'd try to buy the Empire State Building for you if you asked for it. This is a once-in-a-lifetime opportunity. You just gotta work it, sistah!"

Christa couldn't help but laugh. Real, genuine laughter.

"Work it, huh? I'm not sure I know how to do that."

FLIPPING

"Never fear!" said Jadelynn. "That's why you've got me!"

✢ ✢ ✢

Wynson was working on his AP World History term paper. His computer Skype signal went off, and seeing Christa's avatar pop up, he hurried to answer it.

"How did it go?" He positioned himself so that Christa could read his lips clearly.

"Um, can you come over?" Her face showed little expression on the screen.

Wynson's heart dropped. *That isn't good.*

"Well, if you won't tell me on Skype, I'm coming over right now."

"Yeah, okay."

The whole way over, one thing kept running through Wynson's mind over and over. It was the thought that had plagued him ever since Halloween. There was obviously the stumbling, but her personality seemed different too. Was it his imagination or was she more moody, sometimes irritable, but more often distant and aloof, staring into space with a vacant look on her face.

It all added up to one thing: brain tumor.

He jammed the accelerator. *Please. Anything but that.*

When he got to the house, he practically ran past Mrs. McMeri and down to Christa's room. Throwing open the door without knocking, he rushed inside. Christa looked up, startled.

"So, what is it?" he demanded.

"Geez! Relax!" she said.

"I don't need to relax. I need to know what's going on!"

Christa bit her lip. "I've got something called Usher syndrome."

Wynson frowned. "What's that?"

"It's a genetic problem. It's why I went deaf."

"Okaaaay..." Wynson said slowly. "So, what does it mean?"

"Well," Christa couldn't look him in the eye, "it's progressive and incurable."

Wynson felt like he was drowning. The room swam around him and he couldn't breathe.

"Basically," she continued, "they don't know how soon, but I'm going to lose my eyesight."

"Thank God!" he said, relief flooding over him.

Christa's face registered shock and disbelief. *"What?"*

"Oh, geez, Christa. I'm sorry, I didn't mean it that way. It's just I thought you had a brain tumor or something. I thought you might *die...*"

Christa blinked. "Well, I'd never thought of it that way. I guess there *are* worse things that it could have been..."

The reality of what Christa had told him began to dawn on him. She was already hearing impaired. She relied on her sight much more than most people. Even though the cochlear implant gave her some hearing, she still read lips.

Would she even be able to communicate if she lost her sight?

Wynson took Christa's hands in his. "No matter what happens," he said, "I'll be here."

❖ ❖ ❖

Instead of dropping her off at the parking lot, Christa's mom got out of the car and walked with her toward the gym. Christa hugged her arms tightly. It was not cold, but she was shivering. They stopped by the entrance. It was a conversation she didn't want to have.

Christa's mother looked at her questioningly. "Are you sure you don't want me to tell him?" she asked.

"No, I'll tell him myself," said Christa.

"Okay, but remember you promised that you would agree to whatever he says. If he thinks it is too dangerous to continue, you're going to listen, right? No arguments."

Christa nodded. "No arguments."

They asked Coach Eugene if they could speak with him privately.

"Sure," he said. "We can talk in my office."

Christa chewed her nails all the way there.

"So," he said, shutting the door, "what can I do for you ladies?"

Christa took a deep breath and explained her diagnosis. Seeing the expression on Coach Eugene's face made Christa feel like her insides were being shredded like paper.

"I don't know if it's the end," she said, her voice faltering. "I know you only have time to train people who have a real chance of making it. And my abilities are just going to go down. I don't know how much longer I will be able to see well enough to perform…"

Eugene stared intently at her face. "Do you want to keep going?"

"More than anything," she said. "This is what I've wanted to do since I was a little girl."

"Then we're going to make sure you can do it for as long as you possibly can."

"Oh, thank you, Coach!" She leaped up and hugged him. When they parted, Christa was surprised to see his eyes welling up. She looked over to see her mother crying too.

Christa felt her chin begin to quiver ominously.

"Damn onions," Coach Eugene said. They all laughed through their tears.

✦ ✦ ✦

True to her word, Jadelynn took the lead in getting a guide dog. She made the case to their father, who, sure enough, was a pushover. Then Jadelynn coaxed Christa into looking at websites covered with pictures of puppies with cocked heads and perceptive eyes, leading their beloved owners. Training the hyperactive little puppies sounded like a difficult process, but also incredibly fulfilling and beneficial to the future owners.

"We can get a puppy after seven weeks of age and attend 'puppy club' meetings to socialize the little guy. Doesn't that sound fun?"

"Sure," said Christa unenthusiastically.

But when the tawny half-Labrador retriever, half-poodle arrived, Christa couldn't help but fall in love with the big-eyed lummox. They named her Gabby. Having light golden fur with brown ears, Gabby proved to be sheer genius at making a mess, but she was also a quick learner.

"We're top of the class in puppy school," boasted Jadelynn, who was spearheading Gabby's training.

The puppy seemed to have an unerring ability to read Christa's mood and would attack her with wet kisses whenever she was feeling low.

Are you going to be my eyes and ears when I'm deaf and blind? Christa wondered, burying her face in Gabby's furry neck. *Will you be my only friend when I have no one else?*

FLIPPING

❖ ❖ ❖

Wynson had one week of break between the end of junior year and summer school. He accompanied his father to LaShawn Goldbern's office once again.

Wynson sat quietly, staring into space while his father drove. His father listened to KFI AM 640; Thompson & Espinosa was on. He would only set the dial on KFI AM 640 and KFWB News Talk 980, saying that listening to talk shows helped him understand American jokes and slang better. He had to admit that his father's use of slang was much more natural nowadays—*much* to his relief.

"What do you say we get some noodles?" his father said, pulling over to park the car by a Vietnamese pho restaurant.

"Oh, why?" Wynson wondered aloud. *Weird. Dad rarely eats out...especially without Mom.*

"I told Mom we wouldn't be home for lunch." His father exited the car and walked straight toward the door. Wynson followed suspiciously.

They sat inside a simple restaurant, redolent with the aroma of Oriental seasonings. A server served them tea right after they sat down.

"We'll have two orders of spring rolls," his father said.

Wynson felt a sense of impending doom. His father was fixated on him with the kind of commanding stare that signaled, *You'd better listen to me.* Wynson's spine stiffened. He suspected that his father was going to talk about his schools and his life plans.

"Wynson," his father finally broke the heavy silence, "you are our only son. I want you to remember that you have the responsibility to uphold the family honor and heritage. Your decisions affect not just you, but the whole family—your mother and me and even your future children."

Wynson didn't like the direction the conversation was heading. "Geez, Dad, I'm just seventeen! I'm a long way from having kids."

"It's not too early for you to be thinking about these things," his father said. "I was not many years older than you are now when I met your mother. Son, deciding who to marry is the biggest decision of your life. This one decision will determine ninety percent of your happiness or misery."

Wynson stared at his plate, steeling himself for the coming lecture.

"I have noticed you spending much time at the McMeris' house."

Wynson's head shot up and his stomach dropped to his feet. *Oh, God! He knew! Was it so obvious? If his father—who was generally clueless about everything—had figured it out, did everyone else know too?* He tried to rein in his runaway thoughts and tune back in to what his father was saying.

"Jadelynn turned out very attractive. I know she is half our people, but she knows nothing about our culture. The background of her biological father is unclear… She doesn't even speak our language." He had made sure Wynson learned Mandarin.

"So what?" shot back Wynson angrily. "Half Chinese isn't good enough? Well, don't worry! We're just friends. Nothing more. So you don't have to keep going with this. I need to go wash my hands." He threw his napkin down on the table and stalked off, leaving his father staring after him.

Wynson tried to calm himself in the bathroom. There was no point in trying to talk to his father. He had his old-fashioned notions and he wasn't going to change them. He knew with a sickening surety that his father would never accept the girl who had won his heart.

But what difference does it really make? he thought. *She'll never see you as more than a friend anyway.* Sighing heavily, he returned to the restaurant. When he got back to the table, he saw that the food arrived. *Thankfully.*

They ate in silence.

"When I'm Sixty-four" by the Beatles came on the radio.

"Your mother will be still beautiful when she is sixty-four," his father said with affection. "Son, I hope you will find a woman like your mother. She has good family, good genes. You find someone like her and you will have good marriage." He smiled with pride.

Truth be told, Wynson was impressed by his parents' marriage. It seemed like more than half of his friends' parents were divorced, but his parents still acted like newlyweds. It sometimes made him cringe, but he had to admit it was the kind of relationship he hoped to have someday. *It's the one thing Dad got right.*

Wynson tried to tell himself that maybe someday he'd find a girl who would meet all his father's expectations, a girl he could love just as much. But deep down, he didn't believe it. He'd found the love of his life way back in the third grade, and every day since had only made him more sure. *There will never be anyone else for me but her. Not ever.*

Christa continued to practice, but with her failing eyesight, she felt like no matter how hard she tried, she was only losing ground.

One day, she was practicing on the uneven bars. *Rhythm, think about rhythm… the pulse of the music's rhythm.* She heard

Coach Eugene's voice in her head.

She searched within for the rhythm, but the muse did not come. She released the bar, flipping and pivoting in the air. On the way down, she realized something was wrong. She couldn't see the bar. Everything was a blur. She extended her hands, hoping she'd happen to make contact. She grasped nothing but air.

Christa's mouth fell open as the floor rushed up at her.

She clumsily landed in a heap.

"Are you okay?" She saw one of the assistant coaches running over to her.

"Uh," she said stupidly. More confused than anything, she didn't feel any pain. The coach extended a rough hand to her and tried lifting her up. At that point, other gymnasts crowded around her or craned their head at her from afar. She tried to rise but felt a stab of pain in her ankle.

"Come on, girl," said the coach. She wrapped her arm around Christa's back and hoisted her up with the help of another gymnast.

"It hurts!" Christa moaned. "Ugh!"

The coach immediately whisked her to the medical clinic. Christa focused on the physical pain, which was easier to bear than the emotional anguish.

She waited in the examining room for the x-ray results. The doctor came in with her mother.

"You're very lucky," the doctor said. "It's just a sprain. It should be good as new in a couple of weeks."

Despite the doctor's optimistic words, her mother's face was grim. She didn't have to say it.

"It's over, isn't it?"

"I'm afraid so, honey."

FLIPPING

❖ ❖ ❖

When she got home, she wouldn't come out for dinner. Jadelynn tried poking her head through the door with a goofy face.

"Hey, champ," she said, but Christa only glared.

"I want to be alone," she said flatly. Christa was lying spread-eagled on the bed with her ankle propped up. She hated looking at it.

Jadelynn frowned. "Okay. Okay." She closed the door.

Christa stared at the Shawn Johnson poster, the poster she'd looked at every night before she turned off her bedside lamp. Now it mocked her. *You'll never be up here*, it seemed to say. Christa buried her head in her pillow and cried herself to sleep.

❖ ❖ ❖

The bell rang and Wynson headed toward the school cafeteria. Suddenly, Jadelynn was yanking playfully on his backpack.

"Hey, dude!" she said. "How's it hanging?"

"Fine last I checked." Jadelynn was in high spirits, even for her. "Hey, how's Christa? She isn't returning any of my texts or Skypes or emails."

A cloud passed over Jadelynn's face. "She's not doing so hot. She won't come out of her room. She's even convinced our parents to let her stay home 'til her ankle's better, so I'm bringing her assignments. I don't know *how* she pulled that one off!"

"I wish there was something we could do for her," Wynson said. "I can't imagine what she's going through."

"I know. It's just not fair. She's already had more than her share of problems."

"I guess all we can do is make sure she knows we're there for her," Wynson said.

That Friday night, Wynson texted Christa a frantic message: "Contact me ASAP! Urgent!"

A couple of minutes later, his phone vibrated.

"What is it? What's wrong?" Christa demanded in text message.

"You haven't communicated with me in over a week."

"Oh, is that all?"

"All? Yes, that is *all*. We're supposed to be friends, Christa. Friends don't ignore friends. Friends don't leave friends hanging."

"Okay! Okay! I get it! I guess I've been kind of self-absorbed lately. Sorry."

"All right, maybe there's a way you can make it up to me."

"Yeah, what?" she texted back suspiciously.

"Let me take you to the beach tonight."

"The beach?"

"It's on your list. Watch the sun set on the beach. C'mon. It's a beautiful night. I bet the sunset will be gorgeous."

"Why can't you just let me sulk in peace?" Christa replied. "I'm much happier being miserable."

"Well, I'm afraid I'm bound and determined to make you happy, no matter how miserable that makes you."

Christa groaned, then texted, "All right, *fine*. You win!"

Wynson picked her up and they rode in companionable silence. Between her poor night vision and the sprained ankle, Christa had to lean on him to make it down to the beach. Not that he minded.

FLIPPING

It was early fall. The beach was unusually quiet. Wynson pulled out the blanket from his backpack and spread it on the ground. They took a seat. Christa took off her sandal and played with the sand with her toes. The gentle lapping of the waves seemed to have a calming effect on her.

The sun was already near the horizon, turning the sky a beautiful pink-purple. While Christa watched the spectacular natural light show, Wynson watched her.

"You know, I guess it's true what they say," she said wistfully. "You never know what you have until it's gone. I never really appreciated all the beauty that is out there until I realized I'd never see it again."

"You don't know that. You might not lose all your vision for twenty years. You may *never* lose it all."

"Or I might lose it all before next year. But you know what? It really isn't all the things I'll never see. Sure, I want to see the Grand Canyon and the Eiffel Tower. But if I never see them in person, it's not the end of the world. It's seeing *people* I'll miss most. To never see my parents' faces or my sister get married…" She got choked up.

Wynson took her hand and pulled her closer.

"But you know what's even worse?" she continued. "The people I haven't met yet. I'll *never* get to see their faces! I won't even be able to see them in my mind's eye. They'll just be weird, faceless blobs."

Wynson frantically tried to come up with something—anything—comforting to say. He spoke into the microphone of her cochlear implant mindfully.

"Well, think of it this way. You can imagine them however you want. You won't be a slave to looks anymore, like the rest of us poor schmucks. Haven't you always complained about how superficial that is? Now you'll be completely free of it. You can see people for what's inside."

Christa arched an eyebrow.

He sighed. "You're right. That's a stretch."

"Wynson," she said softly, suddenly sounding like a little girl. "I'm scared. Really scared."

"I know."

"I'm afraid I'm going to be trapped in a dark, silent world for the rest of my life. All alone."

Wynson had never wanted anything in his life as much as he wanted to take away Christa's pain. But there was nothing he could say to make it all better.

As the last sliver of sun sank beneath the horizon and Wynson watched Christa's face disappear in the fading light, he imagined that he, too, was going blind. That this was the last time he would ever see her face. How desperate he'd be to save that image, to memorize it for all time. Suddenly he had an idea.

"Hey," he said excitedly. "You know what we should do? We should make a list of all the things you want to see and start ticking them off—you know, sort of like a bucket list."

"I'm going blind, not kicking the bucket," Christa pointed out.

"Okay, how about the *black* list?" he countered.

"Perfect," she said dryly.

And thus, the Black List was born.

Christa was slow to warm up to the idea. She had been so focused on gymnastics, she couldn't think outside the four walls of the gym. She didn't even know what was out there *to* see. At first, Wynson and Jadelynn—who was happy to get in on the action—had to take the lead.

First, they revisited all the famous Los Angeles tourist sites: the Chinese theater, the Walk of Fame, and of course, the iconic Hollywood sign. They gawked at the dinosaur exhibit at the LA Natural History Museum, went to see Monet's *Sunrise* and Van Gogh's *Irises* at the Getty, and posed with their favorite celebrities at the Hollywood Wax Museum.

"I guess this is as close to seeing George Clooney as I'll ever get," Christa joked.

They drove the Pacific Coast Highway, the San Gabriel Canyon Road, and Mulholland Drive; they re-watched all of Christa's favorite movies and visited the zoo and tried to communicate with all the different animals in their own languages.

The more things they did, the more things there *were* to do. The list started to grow longer and longer.

"What about the chalk street painting festival in Pasadena?" Christa said eagerly. "And the New Year's parade in Chinatown? And the surfing U.S. Open?" Wynson was glad to see her excited about something again, to see her looking forward to the future.

"Oh," Christa continued, "and I've always wanted to see a dolphin show, and go to one of those butterfly exhibits where you're just *surrounded* by butterflies! Wouldn't that be amazing? Do they have one of those around here?"

"I'll find one," Wynson promised.

He knew they were in a race against time. How much longer did they have left? Would she get to see the Rose Garden in full bloom in the spring? A baseball game at Dodger Stadium? The Pageant of the Masters in July or the Festival of Chariots in August?

✤ ✤ ✤

At Christmastime, they saw the *Nutcracker* at Dolby Theatre.

Then, a couple of weeks later, they went to the Christmas boat parade at Newport Beach. Jadelynn was spellbound by the sight of the vessels adorned in jewel-like Christmas lights.

"Look at all the trees on the water!" she cried, pointing to the masts decorated like Douglas firs. When the starbursts of light flooded the pier at the end of the parade, Jadelynn whipped her arm in that direction.

"Fireworks! Let's go see 'em!"

It was already dark and Wynson looked at Christa nervously. Sure enough, she kept tripping.

"Let's hold hands," Wynson suggested. "Jadelynn, get on the other side of Christa."

They tightly grasped one another's hands as the crowds pushed and rushed to get to the fireworks. When the fireworks burst into the sky, Wynson glanced at Christa. Her face was a mixture of awe and sadness.

He knew what she was thinking… *Is this the last time I will ever see this?*

✤ ✤ ✤

"It's about time I got you to go shopping," teased Jadelynn as they entered the mall. "I think you're still wearing clothes from middle school!"

"Well, if they still fit, why not? That'll be one upside to going blind. No more clothes shopping!"

Although she appreciated the creativity Jadelynn invested in her wardrobe, Christa couldn't care less about fashion. It didn't help that Christa could still shop in the children's department, while Jadelynn had the tall, willowy physique that the entire female population aspired to and clothes manufacturers adored.

"It'll be your job to dress me," Christa continued. "If you really want to be a clothes designer, it'll do you good to experience firsthand what it's like for us mere mortals who don't have perfect bodies."

"Oh, *please*," Jadelynn retorted. "Do you know how many girls would kill for a body like yours? Totally fit and toned, not an ounce of fat anywhere…"

"…or a curve," Christa finished wryly.

Jadelynn rolled her eyes. "C'mon. We're going to find you something that rocks." They went into Forever 21 and each girl picked out an armful of outfits to try on.

Sure enough, Christa was swimming in the first dress she tried on. "I look like I'm ten," she complained, peeking down at the baggy bodice.

"I know you're self-conscious about your size, but bigger clothes aren't going to make *you* look bigger," said Jadelynn. "Don't hide your body; flaunt it." She grabbed Christa by the hand and led her back out to the floor. "I know *exactly* what you need," she said, marching over to a rack of plain black dresses.

"But these are so boring!" objected Christa. "I need prints or details or something…"

"Trust me," said Jadelynn, pulling one of the dresses off the rack and pushing Christa toward the dressing room. "Put that on and I'll go find some accessories."

When Christa came back out, Jadelynn beamed at her. "Here, try this," she said, tying a scarf around Christa's neck and clipping a wide bracelet on her wrist. She stepped back to observe her handiwork.

"Perfect! You are *so* channeling Audrey Hepburn right now."

Christa looked in the mirror. *Not half bad,* she had to

admit. "Okay, I guess I can trust you not to make me look like an idiot."

"Huh!" Jadelynn scoffed. "I'll make you look *fabulous*, dahling."

"Excuse me?" a man with an olive-green, button-down Oxford shirt interrupted them.

"Yes?" said Jadelynn.

"I'm Christopher Harlow. I'm an agent at ECL Modeling and Talent agency. We have offices in L.A., New York, and Chicago. Here, let me give you a card." While he pulled out his business card, Jadelynn and Christa exchanged an amused glance. "We've been searching for a young lady like you for a while," he said to Jadelynn, giving her his card. "What's your name?"

Of course it's Jadelynn he wants, Christa thought. Jadelynn's ambiguously exotic appearance always turned heads, even more now that she'd lightened her long hair with highlights.

"That's a lovely name," he said when Jadelynn introduced herself. Suddenly, he stopped. "Your eyes!" he said excitedly. "They look like shimmering gold. I've never seen anything like it. Please call me and we can set up a time to discuss details. We're located at North Hollywood. You or your parents can also check out our agency online and on the Better Business Bureau. I can assure you that we are a reputable company. I can even give you some working models' names for reference, if you'd like."

After impressing upon Jadelynn once again how much he wanted her to call, he finally walked away, leaving the girls staring after him.

"What do you think?" Jadelynn asked once he was out of sight.

"Seems legit," said Christa. "I mean, I didn't get any

weird stalker vibe or anything, did you?"

"He seemed respectable," she said, shrugging.

Christa grinned. "Jade, I think you were just 'discovered'!"

"I don't want to be a model, but still, how cool is that?" They dissolved into disbelieving giggles. Jadelynn pulled out her cell phone.

"You calling Mom?"

"No, I want to tell Wynson I was scouted!"

"Oh," said Christa. "Well… I guess I'll go change." When she brought the dress out, Jadelynn didn't see her. She was still animatedly chatting on the phone.

Christa took the dress back to the rack. For some reason, she didn't feel like buying it anymore.

✤ ✤ ✤

One evening, Christa was working on her math homework after gymnastics practice when Jadelynn knocked on her door. Gabby stood up and wagged her tail. Jadelynn poked her head in.

"Hey, Christa, can I talk to you about something?"

"Sure," she said, eager for any excuse to take a break from her sums. She slammed the book shut. "What's up?"

Jadelynn plopped down on the bed. She toyed with her multicolored wristbands and wouldn't meet Christa's eyes.

"Jade, what's wrong?"

"There's nothing *wrong*," she said. "It's just I don't quite know how to tell you this."

"Just tell me."

"Okay." Jadelynn took a deep breath. "I Facebooked my birth mom and I just got a message back from her."

"You…you contacted your birth mom through Facebook? When? Why didn't you tell me?"

Christa hardly ever got on Facebook. She thought it was too time-consuming.

"Christa, don't be mad. I wasn't trying to keep it a secret from you. I didn't want *anyone* to know. I had to tell Mom, of course, but I didn't want to tell anyone else because I didn't want everyone asking if I'd gotten a reply yet and feeling sorry for me if she never wrote back." Tears welled up in Jadelynn's eyes. "If I'd have told anyone, I'd have told you! You're not just my sister; you're my best friend. You know that, right?"

Christa softened, seeing how upset her sister was. She realized with a start that she'd been so caught up in her problems, she hadn't even thought that Jadelynn might be struggling with her own. *Some sister you are.*

"It's okay," Christa said. "I understand. I'm sorry I never even asked you about it. I mean, you're so much a part of the family that I don't even think about you being adopted, but *of course* you'd be curious about your birth parents. I guess I was just too wrapped up in myself to even think about it…"

"Are you kidding?" Jadelynn protested. "It's not your fault. You've got enough on your plate! I knew if I wanted to talk about it, I could always have talked to you. I just wasn't ready yet."

"Good, 'cause you're my best friend too. I wouldn't want anything to ever come between us."

"Me either."

"So, holy crap! That's exciting. You said she wrote back? What did she say?"

Jadelynn's eyes lit up. "She told me how glad she was to hear from me and how she'd always wondered what my life was like but that she knew Mom would be a great mother for me. She's got two kids of her own now and a husband, and they don't know about me. But she wants to keep communicating and maybe someday she'll even come to America to see me!"

"Wow, you couldn't have hoped for anything better than that. That's awesome! I'm so happy for you."

"It never would have happened if it wasn't for Wynson," Jadelynn said.

"Wynson?" Christa said, more sharply than she intended.

"Yeah, it was his idea that I searched her on Facebook. He's such a good guy. You know, I always thought getting nervous and having butterflies in your stomach was the sign you were in love with someone," mused Jadelynn. "But maybe I was wrong. Maybe it's being totally comfortable with someone, being able to be yourself…"

Christa felt her heart constrict.

"We've known each other so long, I never really thought about him that way, y'know? He was just Wynson. Like a brother. But suddenly I'm seeing him in a new light. And, you know, he's a little hard to read, but I think he might like me too. What do you think? Can you see me and Wynson together?"

Christa felt like she'd been sucker punched. It was all she could do to keep her face from registering the shock she felt. All those years of holding her emotions in check for gymnastics stood her in good stead. Jadelynn continued on, seeming not to notice her sister's distress.

"Um, well, he seems… *different* from any of the other guys you've been with," Christa said carefully.

"I know," said Jadelynn. "But maybe that's what I need. Maybe I should at least give it a chance with someone who's more of a friend. Going out with the guys who give me that rush sure hasn't been working! We end up driving each other crazy. I can't see Wynson ever getting like that, can you?"

"No," said Christa. "I think he'd be the perfect boyfriend."

Jadelynn shrugged. "Well, we'll see."

✤ ✤ ✤

For Valentine's Day, Wynson got the girls tickets to Cirque du Soleil.

"You shouldn't have," said Jadelynn. "They're so expensive!"

Too expensive for just a friend, Christa thought. She'd been analyzing Wynson's every move for clues about his feelings for Jadelynn. They obviously enjoyed each other's company, but was that all it was? Or was Wynson's teasing actually flirting? Did his eyes linger on Jadelynn a split second too long? Did he seem annoyed when she mentioned other boys? Christa just couldn't tell.

"You two should go by yourselves," Christa told Jadelynn the night of the performance. "I don't think I'm up for it. I really want to get back to my gymnastic practice." In truth, she was in the blackest mood she'd ever been in.

I am a miserable lost soul without gymnastics.

"You'll only feel worse if you are alone. I know you don't feel like it, but if you force yourself to go out have fun, I guarantee you'll feel better," said Jadelynn. "Besides, you can't bail now. It's too late to find someone else for the ticket."

Christa sulked all the way to the circus as Wynson and Jadelynn made pleasant chitchat, seemingly oblivious to the angry troll glowering at them from the backseat.

FLIPPING

Who wouldn't love Jadelynn? She's always so bubbly and fun. Not like me.

As they walked to the theater, Christa took note of each time Wynson laughed at something Jadelynn said, how close he stood to her, when his hand grazed her arm. *You've got to stop this,* she told herself sternly. *If he likes her, he likes her, and you should be happy for them.*

When Wynson offered to get them popcorn and Cokes, Christa managed a weak smile. "No, thanks. I start on a strict gymnastics diet today."

"Christa, here. I have the flashlight." Wynson pulled out a flashlight, gently touched Christa's elbow, and guided the way.

How could he know it would be too dark for me to see? Christa felt a rush of warmth. However, those sweet feelings dissipated instantly when she noticed Jadelynn holding Wynson's other arm.

They found their seats third row from the front. Although Christa would have preferred to sit between Wynson and Jadelynn, Wynson took that spot, holding the popcorn for the three of them.

The theater filled up quickly. Christa could not carry any conversation with all the background noises. Besides, she couldn't think of anything funny or interesting to say, so instead she shoved handfuls of popcorn in her mouth while Jadelynn kept up a steady stream of animated chatter.

They obviously enjoy each other.

Christa was relieved when the stage lights finally illuminated and the show began so she could stop trying to put on a happy face and indulge her funk in private. But as soon as the first act began, Christa's foul mood evaporated as she found herself riveted by the visual spectacle before her. It was almost as if she was a little girl again, watching the 2008 Olympics and seeing the athletes push their bodies to the absolute limit. Each act was more amazing than the last.

A contortionist twisted into mind-boggling shapes; women in fantastic feathered costumes spun in aerial hoops; a troop of young acrobats performed a synchronized juggling act with ropes and balls. As an elite gymnast, Christa had even greater appreciation for the skill and artistry involved. However, it was an act near the end that really took Christa's breath away. A group of sinewy performers wrapped silk blindfolds over their eyes and began tightrope walking— even swinging from the wires like a human slingshot.

When the act was over, she turned to Wynson, her eyes still wide in awe. "That's no different from gymnastics," she whispered, gripping his hand in excitement.

"Maybe... maybe Coach Eugene can train me *blindfolded*."

✤ ✤ ✤

When Christa told Coach Eugene about her idea, he was skeptical at first. "I don't know anything about training blindfolded," he said.

"What, are you afraid to try something new?" she challenged.

"C'mon, now that we know it is possible, we just have to learn how to do it."

At her insistence, he finally gave in and called the circus to speak to one of the trainers. After a long conversation and an offer to come visit a practice session, Coach Eugene was cautiously optimistic. They gave him some training directions, but more importantly the confidence it could be done, and done safely.

First, he lowered the balance beam to three inches above the floor.

"Let's work on your balance and spatial awareness first."

Christa wrapped the blindfold around her neck with a snug knot and concentrated on Coach Eugene's words. "You need to see with your mind's eye. Find your center of gravity with your core. Use your mental eyes to feel your spatial orientation." He nodded, and she pulled the blindfold over her eyes. With no sound or sight to sway her, she curled her toes around the smooth wood of the beam before taking off into new, dark territory.

For the first time since her diagnosis, Christa felt a ray of hope. Before, she'd been playing catch-up, trying to compensate for the vision loss she'd experienced, always knowing it would only be worse in the next weeks and months. Now she was getting *ahead* of the disease. Once she learned to perform blind, there was nothing else it could take from her. Then she'd be invulnerable. It would be hard, but if all it took was dedication and commitment, then Christa knew she had those in spades.

Watch out, world. I'm back in the game.

❖ ❖ ❖

"Hey, Christa, wait up!" Wynson called from down the hall.

He hurried to catch up with her and touched her shoulder to get her attention.

"When do you want to meet for the parade? Remember, the Chinese New Year is this weekend."

"Oh, uh, I can't make it," Christa said.

"But... it's on the list."

FLIPPING

"Yeah, well, I'll be training all weekend. I have to get back in shape since I've been out of practice for a couple of months *and* learn to do everything blindfolded. I'm going to be training twenty-four/seven if I have any chance at the Olympic trials."

"Oh, uh, okay."

"Maybe Jade would want to go," Christa said. "She's into Chinese culture. I'm afraid I'm not going to have any time for things like that anymore. I've got gymnastics now."

Chapter 9

A s spring approached, a debilitating plague of senioritis swept over the entire twelfth grade class. Many students were so busy dreaming about college that they were already starting to disengage from high school life. But Wynson couldn't seem to get excited about his future plans. LaShawn Goldbern had gotten him a summer internship with a law practice in San Jose. It was an excellent opportunity normally reserved for second- and third-year law school students, but all Wynson seemed to be able to think about was what he would be leaving behind.

One afternoon, he and Jadelynn were in the middle of their usual tennis match, the banter and trash talk flying back and forth between them faster than the ball.

"You'd better pay attention," Jadelynn teased when he failed to return her signature "snap" serve. "You've only got a little while longer to learn everything I have to teach you. Then you're on your own!"

She's right, he thought as he went to retrieve the ball. *There's not much time left. It's now or never.*

At the end of practice, he wiped the back of his hand across his damp forehead.

"Good game, Wynson," Jadelynn said with a smirk,

thinking about her win.

"For you, anyway." Wynson crinkled his nose before bouncing the tennis ball one more time and cracking it against the wire fence.

"Consider this a lesson in humility."

They continued to banter until Wynson abruptly changed the subject. "So, you ready for prom?"

Jadelynn tossed her ponytail coyly. "Oh, you know me. I've got a line of contenders already vying for my hand. Why, is there someone you want to ask?"

He felt the blood rush to his face. "Uh, no. I was just thinking about it. Student council president and all."

"Oh," she said, looking at him curiously.

"Well, I gotta go," he said. "See ya, Jadelynn."

"Yeah, see you later, Wynson."

Christa got home late that evening; she hadn't been able to drag herself away from the gym any earlier. *Just one more*, she'd thought after every routine. She couldn't believe how well her training was going. It was beyond her wildest dreams. Slowly but surely, she had regained all the strength and stamina she'd lost in the months she'd been away from the gym, but her progress didn't end there.

There was no question about it: she was *better* than before. Better than she ever had been. It was the blindfolded practice. It honed her balance, her concentration, her ability to center herself. And those skills didn't go away when she took the blindfold off either.

Everyone should train this way, she thought, but she wasn't about to give away her new secret weapon.

FLIPPING

First my ears, then my eyes, she thought wryly, kicking off her shoes in the foyer. *They keep taking things away, and it only makes me stronger.*

Jadelynn poked her head out of her bedroom. "Hey, sis! How was practice?"

"Really good. I'm doing so much better on the uneven bars. You know that's always been my weakest element. But now I'm so much steadier, and I'm sticking all my landings. And Coach Eugene is working on my Amanar vault. I was able to back handspring onto the vault table and off-flight high, hold my body tight, and make a two and a half twists; the landing was kind of sloppy still, but I am working on it." Christa could not hold her exhilaration. Her spirits were high. "I'm thinking I might really have a chance at the Olympic trials after all. If my vision can just hold out for a while..."

"I bet it will. Your last appointment went so well; your vision has barely changed since you were first diagnosed. I bet you have years and years till it gets really bad."

"You know what they say about how unpredictable it is. You just never know," said Christa, shrugging. "So what about you? How was tennis practice?"

Jadelynn bit her lip. "Actually, I wanted to talk to you about that. You know that Wynson and I have been hanging out a lot lately."

Christa's stomach tightened. Of course she knew. They'd been doing all the things on her list that she didn't have time for. They always invited her along, but it was just a formality. They knew she was too busy with gymnastics.

"Well, today at practice," Jadelynn continued, "Wynson said something about prom and then he started acting sort of weird. I think he might have been trying to see if I would be open to the idea of going to prom with him. But then he dropped it. I don't know if he's afraid I'll say no or he doesn't want to ruin the friendship or he's afraid it would upset you or what."

"Why would I care?" Christa said, doing her best to feign nonchalance.

"I didn't think you would, but since the three of us always hang out, maybe he's afraid you'd feel left out or something. You're sure it wouldn't bother you if we got together?"

Every cell of Christa's body rebelled at the thought. But another voice asked: What right did she have to keep them apart? How she could stand between the two people she loved most in the world if they could make each other happy?

"Wynson's a great guy. You'd be good together. Of course, I don't mind," Christa lied.

❖ ❖ ❖

"Ready to get your butt handed to you?" Wynson teased, taking a practice swing on his racket.

"I think someone needs a lesson in humility," Jadelynn shot back.

"You're dragging today, McMeri," Wynson said as the balls kept flying past her.

Jadelynn flexed her hand before gripping her racket tighter. "Every athlete has her rough days."

"What was that about a lesson in humility?" Wynson crowed when he won the match handily 6-0.

"Har, har. Anyway, whenever you get a chance later, I have something for you to read." Jadelynn tucked a piece of paper in the front pocket of Wynson's racket bag before hurrying away.

He curiously retrieved and unfolded the note.

FLIPPING

Wynson,

I've been thinking about it since your epic defeat, after you mentioned prom. You know I'm not one to play games (besides tennis). SO, I wanted to say that I'd love it if you were my prom date. Not only that, but maybe something more.

You've always been a great friend. Some of my best memories are with you. I hope our prom is the start of something awesome.

Jadelynn

Wynson stared at the note in disbelief, his insides twisted into knots. How had he gotten himself into this mess? All that time he'd spent with Jadelynn so he could get closer to Christa—was it any wonder she got the wrong idea? Surely, he told himself, Jadelynn couldn't be too serious about him. She always had a string of boys after her, and she was never hung up on any of them for long.

This is a passing thing, just like all the others. It had to be.

❖ ❖ ❖

Wynson agonized over how to answer Jadelynn's letter. He knew he didn't have long to decide. They'd see each other the next day at school. While he thought it would probably be better to reply to her face-to-face, he simply couldn't do it.

By writing her back, he told himself, it would allow her to deal with the rejection in private.

FLIPPING

Jadelynn,

Wow, I definitely appreciate your kind words. You're much braver than me.

It's hard to say this, but I have to be honest (just like you were honest with me). There is somebody else in my heart.

Sorry for any mixed signals on my end. But I still love you in another way, and I hope we won't ever let anything get in the way of our friendship.

Wynson

He slipped the note to her in person, right before school let out and she was heading to her mother's car. He couldn't bear seeing her reaction, so he kept his head down.

✢ ✢ ✢

"Oh, my God! I'm so embarrassed!" Jadelynn wailed, flopping dramatically onto Christa's bed.

Jadelynn pushed the crumpled paper toward Christa. Christa quickly scanned the note.

"Oh, sis, I'm so sorry," Christa said, cursing the traitorous heart that was doing leaps and spins in her chest. *There is somebody else in my heart. Could it be?!?*

"Somebody else? Who on earth could that be?" Jadelynn asked. "In all the years we've known him, I've never seen Wynson interested in any other girl. I've gone over every girl at school and there isn't one that he's ever paid even the slightest attention to. Have you *ever* heard him talk about a girl or do anything to make you think he had a crush on someone?"

Christa shook her head.

"Unless..." Suddenly Jadelynn sat bolt upright. "That's it!"

"What? What's it?"

"Of course! I don't know why I didn't see it before!" Jadelynn said, smacking her forehead.

"What?"

Jadelynn smiled triumphantly. "He's *gay*."

Christa gulped as the roller coaster of her emotions took another heart-stopping plunge. "Gay?"

"It all makes sense. Why he's never gone out with anyone. Why he never talks about girls. Why his best friends are women. Think about it: if he liked a *girl*, why not just ask her out? Why all the secrecy? His parents are pretty traditional. It's probably totally unacceptable for him to be gay."

This revelation seemed to improve Jadelynn's mood considerably, but it crushed Christa. As much as she hated to admit it, though, what Jadelynn said made sense. Wynson had always been "one of the girls." He was easy to talk to, even about emotional things, and he never looked at girls the way even the *nice* guys did. It was like he didn't even see them. It had been wishful thinking to imagine—if only for a second—that he liked *her*.

❖ ❖ ❖

Wynson was surprised at how easily Jadelynn seemed to get over his rejection. He'd been afraid it would ruin their friendship, or cause some awkwardness between them at the very least. But Jadelynn came right out and told him she didn't take it personally and she only wanted him to be *happy*.

"I hope you'll be able to be with the person you talked about in your note," she said. "Love is the most important thing in life. You can't let anything stand in your way."

Even though he didn't think Jadelynn knew who he'd meant, Wynson still felt like he'd gotten a sort of blessing—if not a command—from her. *I've got to do it. I've got to tell her.*

⚜ ⚜ ⚜

One day when Jadelynn was home sick with a cold, Wynson gave Christa a ride home. The whole drive, he kept trying to work up the courage to tell her, but he just couldn't find the right words. He used his peripheral vision to glance at her.

Christa was completely silent; she stared frontward, as still as a statue. Her mind was afflicted by a series of incidents in the last few days. First, she had bumped right into two students who stood still in the parking lot talking; that was under the bright daylight. Then, she tripped over Gabby. That morning, she had sat across the dining table from Jadelynn at breakfast and she saw only part of Jadelynn's face; it was like looking at her through a paper tube. She recalled rolling paper into a tube and looking through it, pretending to be a pirate when she was little. That's how Jadelynn's face looked!

They said I would have tunnel vision! It's happening now. I am going blind. It's a reality now. I must keep it to myself. It's a secret. I will tell nobody, not my parents, not Jadelynn, not Coach Eugene, not even Wynson. Christa had made up her mind.

All too soon, they pulled up to her house. Wynson turned off the engine. *It's now or never.*

"Do you have a date for prom?" He faced her squarely and asked as casually as he could.

"No, I don't plan on going." Christa tilted her head down slightly so she could see his mouth. She was disturbed again that she could not see his whole face.

"Why?"

"Well, no one asked me for starters."

"Christa, I'd like *you* to be my prom date. Would you go with me?"

Christa frowned. "You don't have to feel sorry for me. I probably wouldn't enjoy it anyway. I can't hear well in crowds and it will probably be dark…"

"I'm not asking for you." He reached out to hold her hand gently and surprised her with that move. "I'm asking for me. I want to go to prom with you. I know we'd have a great time. Please go with me."

"I'll definitely think about it," she finally said after a long pause. She exited the car and gave him a small smile before heading inside to compensate for her lack of an answer.

✛ ✛ ✛

"Of *course* you should go!" Jadelynn exclaimed when Christa told her about Wynson's invitation. "It's prom. You *have* to go to prom. It's, like, a requirement for graduation or something."

Christa couldn't make up her mind. Of course, she would love to go with Wynson, but would she just be torturing herself being that close to someone she could never have? Would it be just one more time where she was on the outside, looking in?

It's cruel to desire something that does not belong to me…

"Just because you don't have a boyfriend doesn't mean you shouldn't go," Jadelynn continued. "There's nothing wrong with going with a friend. I'm not that into Roland either. But he's a lot of fun and there won't be any drama. You and Wynson will have a blast, I know it. And besides, if you don't go, it will ruin *my* prom! It wouldn't feel right not having you there."

"Oh, all right," Christa said, groaning. "Twist my arm, why don't you?"

With her sister's prodding, Christa accepted Wynson's invitation.

❖ ❖ ❖

"What do you say about going to the LA fashion district to shop for prom dresses?" their mother offered, leaning against the doorway of Christa's room as both of the girls chatted on the floor with magazines fanned around them, the smiles of celebrities radiating from their glossy front pages.

The girls looked at each other suspiciously before looking up. "Really?"

"Your senior prom only happens once. C'mon."

With that the girls scrambled to put on their shoes and grab their purses. In no time, they were strolling along the sunny sidewalks and taking a gander at the sample sales at each stand. All in all, everyone seemed to be in great spirits as they walked by and perused the stores.

Jadelynn knew what she wanted to wear as soon as she saw it on Santee Alley. The forest-green, sequined dress reminded her of a mermaid, and she laughed as everyone recalled her childhood fantasy.

Christa didn't have Jadelynn's fashion sense, so she relied on her sister's eye. They passed a mannequin that Christa walked right past, but Jadelynn swooped to its side like a magnet.

"Oh, this is pretty! I think it would bring out your eyes." Jadelynn motioned for her sister to stand beside the creation: a royal blue, A-line, V-neck sleeveless chiffon dress. It was a little below knee length. "I admit I like the appeal of not tripping over a long dress all night."

"Try it on!" their mother encouraged, rummaging in her purse for a camera phone.

With permission granted, Jadelynn snatched it off the hanger and helped Christa along to the fitting room. As soon as she put it on, they both knew: it was the one.

When Christa came out and stood on the pedestal, their mother gasped. "My little girl! You look so beautiful." A bead of a tear sat in the corner of her eye.

Christa stood regally, like a statuette, her toned shoulders beautifully framing her collarbone. Her eyes were like two blue beacons. The waves of the dress gracefully rolled down her knees, and when she moved, it was dynamic as the ocean.

"What do I do?" she asked, laughing. She put both arms in the air as if she had just stuck a landing in a gymnastics competition.

Her mother snapped the picture just in time.

Wynson came home from the shop with his tux. He could still barely believe it. *I'm going to prom with Christa!* True, it wasn't an actual *date*, but it was a step in the right direction. Surely the dance would present the perfect time to make his feelings known. They would be swept up in the romance of the evening and...

He was so engrossed in his thoughts, he almost didn't see

his father sitting on the living room couch, flipping through a finance magazine. When he did see him, though, he suddenly knew that he had been waiting there for a while—it was time for another "I am your father, I have been around much longer than you have, I know what I am talking about, you don't know what you are doing, I don't want you to ruin your life, you have to listen to me" speech.

As if on cue, his father put down the magazine and said, "Son, sit down. We need to talk."

Wynson did as he was told and braced himself.

"I do not mind you are going to prom with Christa. She is a nice girl—very accomplished with the gymnastics, especially being deaf. But I do not want you to have a serious relationship with her. You should date girls like you."

Wow, Wynson thought. *He's never one to mince words.*

His father continued with a face of stone, with his hands resting on his knees. He was like a powerful Chinese emperor of old. "You need to think in long term and the consequence of your action. You know there is no future in this relationship. You should not give her false hopes. You want to marry a woman with good genes, not someone with birth defect… think about your future generations. You do not want to risk having bad genes in your children or generations to come. Can you bear the pain and responsibilities of having a birth-defect child? You have seen the difficulties Christa deals with in her daily life. Why can't you go out with girls like your mother? Your mother is a good woman, smart and has good genes.

"Haven't you ever watched the Kennel Competition or horse racing? You know a good breed is the key to be a champion… You have the responsibility to preserve the integrity of your genetic makeup…"

FLIPPING

His father just kept going on and on.

Wow! How long did it take him to come up with these scripts? They're sounding more and more absurd!

Wynson's friends always commended him that his parents were "un-Asian" parents—not too strict or traditional. His father even allowed him to invite friends to the house for a LAN party on his sixteenth birthday. But Wynson couldn't help but feel his father was acting "fresh off the boat" at the moment. He could barely stand it each time he implied Christa was a faulty human because of her "birth defect."

"Dad, I love her," Wynson declared. He was not a person who easily spelled out his feelings to anyone—least of all his father.

His father scoffed. "What do you know about love? My grandparents were engaged while they were still in their mothers' wombs. They were married for fifty-some years and died only a few days apart."

Wynson had heard that story a few times before. His father liked to use his grandparents' marriage to illustrate true love, but it sounded so twisted at the moment. Two good friends' wives got pregnant around the same time, and they vowed that the unborn children would get married at fifteen years old if they were the opposite sex. Wynson tried not to roll his eyes.

"Dad, would they still get married if one of them came out with a birth defect?" Wynson debated with a tone of rebellion.

"I just do not want you to go out with her anymore. Even if you are eighteen years old, you still need to listen to me. You are living in America, but you cannot talk to me like an American boy," his father said heatedly.

FLIPPING

His mother emerged from the bedroom. *"Aiya,* why arguing?" She turned to her husband. "If it comes down to that point, they can adopt. They don't have to have their own kids. Look at Jadelynn."

"He is our only son. We need someone to pass down our bloodline with good heredity," Wynson's father said in Mandarin.

At that point, Wynson simply nodded and escaped to his room.

❖ ❖ ❖

Christa surveyed herself in the mirror. With her constricting tunnel vision, she scanned herself by moving her head from the top and slowly down. Her hair fell in loose curls instead of tightly pinned back into her usual athletic bun or ponytail. The golden strands enhanced her blue eyes, which only deepened with the blue of her dress.

The evening began with a blur of flashing lights from the photographs. They gathered at the McMeris' house for the typical picture of the diagonal line of prom-goers. The prom would take place on the RMS *Queen Mary*, which sat in all its regal glory on the dock of Long Beach. The ocean beside it was like sapphire glass, reflecting the lights from aboard. The excited hollers and laughs of the senior class echoed from the deck. Christa was glad to be able to share this once-in-a-lifetime night with one of her best friends.

"Oh, before I forget," Wynson said, holding up a finger. "I need to go back to the car." When he came back, he had a beautiful stargazer lily corsage for Christa. "Just wanted to give this to you alone. I know it's your favorite flower."

Christa grinned. The night was perfect so far—the air was

crisp and refreshing, but not cold. It was May, after all. Plus, Wynson had remembered her favorite flower—she couldn't recall ever telling him what it was, and if she did, it was a long time before.

"Thanks, not just for that, but everything. Thanks for bringing me here."

"Why would you thank me?" Wynson seemed irritated. "I told you, this isn't a charity date."

Christa made a mental note to not use self-deprecating humor. She didn't know why she used it then since she hardly ever did.

When they entered the banquet room, Christa felt that she was on the *Titanic*. The doors swept open to reveal plush rugs surrounding the polished wood floor, radiant wood paneling, and golden wood columns that enhanced the magnificent history of the ship. Balconies overlooked the luxurious dining area.

"Oh, there you are," said Roland, turning to them and waving. His sandy blond hair defied the power of hair gel; stray hairs fell in his face. Christa wondered how he'd fare after Jadelynn took him for a whirl on the dance floor.

"Well, I don't know about you, but after all those photos I'm ready to boogie," Jadelynn said, grinning broadly at her date. "C'mon!"

As soon as they left, other friends of Wynson and Christa's jumped in. "Hey, we have to take photos!" someone shouted, and the prom pictures started again. They paired off, took guys' pictures, girls' pictures, and more. They flagged down a chaperone so he could take more group photos with their cliques. It wasn't until everyone left to go dance that Wynson stood across from Christa, now looking like a bashful boy in a tux rather than her debonair date.

"What do you say about a dance?" Christa said. She could hardly hear her own voice, feeling heavy bass in the room. She wondered if Wynson wanted to go on the dance floor but was too afraid to pressure her. The music was too loud and the background noises overwhelming; she turned down the volume of her implant processor. It wasn't that she was afraid to dance—she felt the vibrations of the room and smelled the energy in the air.

Wynson's reply was drowned in the blaring music.

"Huh?"

He held her right hand and wrote on her palm, "GO OUTSIDE, OK?"

"Great idea! I bet it's beautiful," she said.

He wrapped his right arm around her waist and his left hand held hers, guiding her out. As soon as they went outside, Christa couldn't help but feel immediately calm. The smell of the ocean and the sense of the waves against the ship was so serene; the gentle breeze caressed her bare skin and the vibration of sound from the music charged the air with electricity. She used her fingers to touch the railing and turned and leaned against it. Christa smiled and adjusted her CI processor volume again.

"Christa," Wynson said, suddenly pivoting on his heels to look at her. Then he looked up to adjust his position so the light would fall right on his face and Christa could read him clearly. "I just have to tell you…something."

"What?" Christa asked.

Wynson's hands were awkwardly in front of him, as if he were about to move her somewhere more quiet. He abruptly stuffed them in his pockets and looked at her. Then he pulled his hands out.

"Want to sit down?" He guided her to a bench in front of

a light post near some lifejackets, and Christa took a seat.

Wynson sat beside her on the opposite end of the bench, leaving a comfortable space between them. He faced her squarely. He opened his mouth—shut his mouth—and opened it again. "Christa, there's something I need to tell you," he finally managed.

Oh, my God. He's coming out.

"I'm not as good at this as I thought I'd be." He sighed. "I can't tell you how many times I've rehearsed this, but the words just wouldn't come."

Christa's heart twisted seeing him struggle so. What a terrible burden he'd been carrying all this time, and she hadn't even known it. Her disability was hard, but at least she'd never had to keep her very identity a secret—even from the people who loved her best.

Wynson ran his hand through his hair. "I hope I'm not ruining anything by telling you. That's why I've kept it from you all this time. I couldn't bear the thought of losing you as a friend. But I can't keep it inside anymore. It's eating me alive."

"It's okay, Wynson. You don't have to tell me. I know."

Wynson stopped. "You… know?"

"Yeah," she said. "Jadelynn figured it out. After you wrote her the note."

Wynson stared at her, astonished. "*And?*"

"And I just wish you'd told me earlier!"

A slow smile spread across his face. "Really?"

"Absolutely!" she said, glad she could give him this gift. The thought that anyone would make him feel bad about himself just for being who he was rankled her to no end. He was wonderful exactly the way he was.

Wynson beamed. "You have no idea how happy that

makes me! I don't care *what* my father says; this is all that matters."

Suddenly, Wynson closed the distance between them. Christa thought at first he was coming in for a hug, but instead, before she knew what was happening, he had taken her in his arms and his mouth was on hers, drawing her into a deep, passionate kiss.

Christa's body melted into his and her every atom seemed to hum with life. Then her brain kicked in. She backed up and pushed Wynson away.

"What are you doing?" she asked sharply.

"What, am I moving too fast? I'm sorry. It's just I've been waiting for this for so long, I guess I got carried away..."

Christa shook her head, struggling to understand what was going on. It seemed pretty clear, but she simply couldn't believe it.

"The someone in your heart? In your letter? That was *me*?"

Wynson cocked his head, confused. "Well, yeah. I thought you said you knew. I love you, Christa. I always have. Since the first day we met." He exhaled deeply. "Christa, how I love you..." It was a whisper, but Christa read it clearly.

It can't be true. This isn't happening. Emotions crashed over her like a tsunami. Before she knew it she was running, running like she'd never run before. She flew down the steps and toward the elevator. She ran right into a couple.

"Hey, miss!" the man shouted.

Wynson ran after her. She fell. Wynson caught up with her and helped her up.

"Leave me alone! I just want to go home. Please call my mom to pick me up."

Not to make a scene, Wynson did what she said.

FLIPPING

Christa got up and ran again. Wynson followed at a distance to make sure she was okay.

✤ ✤ ✤

Christa leaned against the wall of the boardwalk shop, waiting for her labored breath and pounding heart to return to some semblance of normal. She couldn't believe she'd just run away like that. What on earth had come over her? Wasn't this what she had always wanted? What she'd fantasized about in the most secret and hidden recesses of her mind, buried so far down she couldn't even admit it to herself?

And now when her most tender, cherished dream had come true, what she felt was sheer, overwhelming panic.

What's wrong with me? Was it just "first time" jitters? Was she afraid of losing Wynson's friendship if things didn't work out? Was she letting her pending blindness overshadow her love for him? Yes, that must be it. Teen romances never lasted and Wynson was far too good a friend to lose. Besides, she had more than enough on her plate, especially with the Olympic trials right around the corner. And they would be leaving for college soon, so why start something that couldn't last? She had to be logical, rational.

Using every shred of her hard-won emotional discipline, Christa stuffed her feelings for Wynson back inside the friendship box and slammed shut the lid.

It may be hard, she thought as she saw her mother's car approaching, *but it's better for everyone this way.*

✤ ✤ ✤

Wynson felt like he was sleepwalking through the rest of the evening. Everything seemed to come at him from a vast distance, as if a chasm separated him and the rest of the world.

Surely, he thought, this was some sort of nightmare from which he would soon awaken.

He replayed the scene over and over. The feel of Christa's body pressed to him, her lips against his. It had been perfect, all he had ever imagined—better, even. They had fit together like they were a matched set. And before she had pulled away, she had returned his kiss, he *knew* she had. What had gone wrong?

He texted Christa repeatedly, but other than a terse message telling him she made it home safely, it had been total radio silence. He considered showing up at her house, and he even got in his car at one point, but his natural reserve won out and he shuffled back to his room, turned out the lights, and blasted mournful love ballads at full volume.

Even his ever-unobservant father noticed Wynson's sorry state. "Are you feeling okay?" he asked when his son didn't eat any of his dinner on Sunday night. "You don't look so good."

"It's nothing," snapped Wynson.

His mother looked at him sympathetically, which for some reason made him even more furious.

"I'm not hungry," he announced abruptly and stalked up to his room.

On Monday morning, he was punch-drunk, having been up all night, tossing and turning and thinking about what he would say to Christa when he saw her. He was dying to see her but terrified too. The fact that she wouldn't respond to his texts didn't bode well.

When he finally saw her, his heart dropped. Her

expression was hard. It was the "game face" she put on before competitions.

"Christa, we need to talk," he said.

"I know," she replied coolly. "We will. At lunch."

❖ ❖ ❖

Christa fought the butterflies in her stomach all morning. She didn't want to talk to Wynson. Just seeing him made her want to forget all her well-intentioned promises and shout, "Yes! Yes, Wynson! I love you too!" She didn't know how she'd manage to keep it together when they spoke.

Just remember, you're doing the right thing.

They met in the parking lot and sat in Wynson's car, where they wouldn't be overheard by passersby.

"Look," Wynson started, "I'm sorry if I came on too strong. I didn't mean to scare you."

"I wasn't scared—just surprised. I shouldn't have run like that. I didn't know what to do."

The hurt look on Wynson's face cut Christa to the quick.

"Was it really that bad?"

"No," she hurried to explain. "Not at all. You're a great guy and I'm flattered that you—"

"Flattered? I don't want you to be *flattered*. So you're saying you don't have any feelings for me?"

Christa couldn't outright lie. "It's not a good idea... us," she said, picking her words carefully.

He frowned. "Not a good idea? What does that mean?"

"It just doesn't make any sense. I've got gymnastics; we'll both be going to college soon..."

"But how do *you* feel about me? *That's* what matters! Geez, you sound like my dad! It's not some business calculation you make to maximize your returns. It may not make sense, but I *love* you, Christa, and I don't care what he says. I want to be with you."

The heat rushed to Christa's face. "What do you mean, what your dad says? He... he doesn't want us to be together?"

Wynson looked away. "You know how he is. He's old school. He wants me to be with someone...Chinese."

There was only the slightest hesitation before "Chinese," but Christa caught it.

"No, that isn't it, is it? He doesn't want you to be with me because... because of how I am, right?"

"It's stupid!" Wynson said forcefully. "It's not just you. He's like that with everything. *Nothing's* ever good enough. He's got to have the best house, the best car, the best son... Believe me, he doesn't think I'm ever good enough either."

Christa wasn't listening. She could barely breathe. It was her biggest fear come true. The single, driving thought that had haunted her all her life, that slithered in beside her in the dark of night, that ambushed her whenever she took a fall or missed the punchline of a joke. Although her parents had always told her she was just as good as anyone else, Christa knew they *had* to say that. They were family. Deep down, she'd never been able to escape the fear that no matter what she did, how nice or kind she was, what she achieved, that on some fundamental level, she was defective. Unworthy of love. Even Helen Keller had never been married; she died alone.

See? the voice taunted. *It's true. You're not good enough. You'll never be good enough. You are the curse of fate.*

Tears welled up in her eyes. She didn't want Wynson to look at her. She didn't want *anyone* to look at her. She grabbed the door handle.

"Look, you can tell him he doesn't have to worry about it. It's not going to happen!"

She opened the door and got one foot out before Wynson grabbed her arm.

"Christa, don't—!"

She took a deep breath and tried to collect herself. She had to preserve whatever vestige of self-respect she had left.

"Look," she said, as calmly as she was able. "I know it's not your fault, but I just can't do this, okay? It's too much. I want you to leave me alone."

"But—"

Christa stopped him. "If you *really* care about me, you'll do this for me."

Wynson stared at her for a long, interminable moment and then a look of deep resignation passed over his face.

"All right," he said softly, releasing her arm. "If that's what you really want."

Christa was barely able to make it out of the car before the tears started to fall.

Chapter 10

Wynson exited the testing hall; he wanted to go back to his dorm to catch a few hours of sleep after a week of sleep deprivation. His friends were throwing a party that night to celebrate surviving the first year at Columbia University. He did not want to miss it just to sleep, even as attractive as it sounded at that moment. His brain was like a washrag that had been wrung out. Two all-nighters later, after giving finals his all, he had nothing left to give.

After he pushed the heavy oak doors open and stepped out into the New York sunlight (a creature of the day once again!), he reached into his backpack to make sure his phone was still there after having it off and ignoring its existence most of the week. He pushed the ON button; his cell phone slowly came alive. He was surprised to see a text message from his dad.

"Call now."

He didn't waste any time. His father had kept close tabs on Wynson's progress when he first got to school—"Did you study enough? Did you feel prepared? You think you got an A?"—but since New Year, there had been virtual silence from both his parents. Wynson took that to mean his father had been satisfied with his first-semester grades and didn't need to monitor him as closely this semester. But he obviously wanted to know how finals went.

After settling on a campus bench placed under a tree, Wynson touched the line "Dad mobile" on his phone screen. After two rings, his father picked up.

"Hi, Dad. It's me." He spoke in Mandarin.

"Are you somewhere quiet? Somewhere safe?"

Wynson raised a brow. *Safe?* His father sounded hoarse, even a bit paranoid. "Um, yeah. I just finished my last final. I'm sitting on a bench."

"There's something I have to tell you about your mother."

When Wynson hung up, he sat back on the bench. *Hereditary diffuse gastric cancer.* The term kept going around and around in his mind. His father had to repeat the name of the disease several times before he could comprehend it. If he was drained before, he was completely empty now. He didn't know how he would will his legs to carry him back to the dormitory. Instead he stared blankly at the students walking by, seemingly unaware that the world had just turned upside down.

He had always heard the phrase that life flipped on a dime. Christa was fond of it.

Christa.

They hadn't spoken since graduation, but she was still the first person on his mind. After prom, Christa had made it painfully obvious that she didn't want anything to do with him, and once school ended, she hadn't responded to any of his many texts or emails or Skypes. Eventually he quit trying.

He'd heard through the grapevine that she hadn't qualified for the Olympics trial, but, fed up with feeling like a pathetic stalker, he'd unfriended her on social media.

However, he could never truly put her out of his mind.

If only she were here with me now...

✤ ✤ ✤

Wynson came home to a mother who was half dead. She was alarmingly thin, and he was afraid to hug her lest he snap her back. He did, though—insisting that she stay in bed, but she got up anyway. She felt like a bag of twigs. Her head was wrapped in a crimson scarf, and he had a sinking feeling when he realized what wasn't underneath.

"I missed you," she said, her voice muffled against his shoulder.

Wynson pulled away and his eyes darted to the side. "Just get back into bed, Mom," he told her. "I'm here."

SuAnn's eyes drooped as she smiled. "I'm so happy you're home. The hospital sent me home and I am under the hospice's care now." She sounded so calm, like she was talking about someone else's business.

Wynson added another blanket to his mother's bed. "Why don't you rest?" he said.

SuAnn closed her eyes obediently, and once she appeared to be sleeping, Wynson slipped into the hall, where he found his father waiting outside the door.

"How on earth could you not have called me sooner?" Wynson hissed quietly so his mother wouldn't hear him. "Don't you think I should have known?"

His father frowned. "We didn't want to upset you. You had your studies to concentrate on..."

"Are you *kidding*? Do you think my schoolwork is more important than being here? You're unbelievable!" With that, he stalked off down the hall.

FLIPPING

Wynson knew that some of his rage was against the disease that was taking his mother, but he didn't care. He was furious. His father didn't know what was important—had *never* known—and he wasn't going to put up with it anymore.

✤ ✤ ✤

In the following days, Wynson spent every waking moment with his mother, which meant having to deal with his father, since he never left her side. Wynson tried not to let his irritation show so as not to upset his mother, but the tension between them was palpable.

One day when his father was in kitchen making lunch, SuAnn called Wynson over to her bedside.

"Wynson," she said, her voice barely above a whisper, "I want to talk with you about your father."

Wynson tried to object, but she silenced him with a finger over his lips.

"I know you're upset with him for not telling you I was sick. But you shouldn't be mad at him. I told him not to tell you."

"I don't care!" protested Wynson. "He should have told me anyway."

"I made him promise. Wynson, he *begged* me to let him call you, but I wouldn't." She gave him an elfin smile. "It just about killed him, but your father has never been able to say no to me. He's been so good to me…"

Hearing his mother praise his father made Wynson mad all over again, but he tried to bite his tongue. He'd only hurt her by attacking the man she so idealized.

"Wynson," she said, taking his hands and drawing him close, "he loves you so much. Can't you please try to be more considerate toward him, for my sake?"

Wynson pulled away. That was too much. "More considerate? How can I be any *more* considerate than I already am? I've bent over backwards my entire life to do what he wants! I was on student council for him. I played tennis for him. I'm in law school for him."

I gave up Christa for him.

"What more do you want from me?" he asked brokenly.

"Wynson, I couldn't have asked for a better son. I'm so proud of you. I want you to live the life that makes you happy. And you may not believe it, but that's all your father wants for you too. Please, Wynson, I want you to make your peace with him. I need to know that my two boys will be there for each other when…" She trailed off.

When I'm not here, Wynson finished silently.

"Of course, Mom," he assured her. "You don't have to worry about that. We'll be fine. I promise." He hoped it sounded genuine.

✤ ✤ ✤

For his mother's sake, Wynson made a real effort to get along with his father—at least in front of her. He had to admit his old man couldn't have been a more attentive nurse. He cooked her the foods she could keep down, managed her medicines, bathed and dressed her, and even took her to the bathroom, all as if it was the most natural thing in the world.

Despite his mother's fragile health, somehow the house didn't feel like a death ward. His parents had a glow he'd never seen before. They were always laughing and touching and holding hands. When his mother was having an especially hard time, his father would put on one of their favorite old movies, *It's a Wonderful Life* or *Casablanca*. It always seemed to calm her down.

Day by day, though, the hard times lasted longer and came closer together and Wynson could see his mother slipping away.

One day when Wynson's father was out refilling her prescriptions, his mother took an intense interest in something outside her window. "What is that?" she asked Wynson.

"What's what?" he asked, craning to see what she was looking at.

"It's a lion out there."

Wynson felt his heart tear in half. There was nothing outside—not even a shaggy dog that could be mistaken for a lion.

"Mother, you're exhausted. Please sleep."

He tried to maneuver her back into bed like he'd seen his father do.

"Darling," she said, gazing at him adoringly, "I'm so lucky to be your wife. You've been so good to me."

"Mom, it's me, Wynson. Your son."

"I love you too," she said, smiling with childlike contentment.

Within seconds she fell asleep.

❖ ❖ ❖

Jadelynn was away at UC Davis studying pre-veterinary. The house was quiet. Christa was in her room, reading with a low vision optical device, when her mother came in. Without a word, Christa could sense something was wrong. She felt a lump in her throat and her stomach tightened.

"Christa…" Her mother sat close to her. "I just got a call from a friend that Mrs. Tang died."

The words struck Christa like a whip. "Are you sure?" she gasped.

"I'm afraid so. It sounds like it was cancer. I feel so awful… I didn't even know she was sick."

Poor Wynson. How terrible for him! She wished there was some way to help him; that he could somehow feel her love from afar.

"Such a tragedy," her mother continued. "She was still so young. It seems like just yesterday we were in the PTA together when you kids were small…" She sighed heavily. "Anyway, the memorial service is Friday. I'm sure you'll want to be there for Wynson. Most of his other friends will probably be off at college. It'll be nice for him to see a few friendly faces there."

The idea of *seeing* Wynson again sent shock waves through Christa's system. In the last year, so much had happened that she was an entirely different person than the girl he had known. The accomplished, fiercely independent girl who knew exactly what she wanted and went after it like a terrier had gone. The girl he'd declared his love for didn't exist anymore.

Would the special connection they had shared still be there?

⁘ ⁘ ⁘

Death warped all sense of time. Wynson felt like it had been years since he last saw his mother, even though it had only been few days. So much about him had changed. But more striking still was his father's transformation. Wynson's father had aged overnight. He shuffled around the house like a ghost and spent much of his time in the study with the door closed. What was once an active man, both physically and mentally, was now a shell.

One evening, Wynson found him in the study alone in the dark again. His father stared outside the window even though there was only blackness outside.

Be more considerate. Be there for each other.

"Dad, are you okay?" Wynson finally asked softly.

"I can feel her in the dark," his father replied. His voice was dead. "Life has flipped me around. I thought I had everything. Now your mother is gone. It's all meaningless." He emitted a loud cry and sobbed.

"It's okay, Dad. I'm here." He went over to hug his father, just like his father hugged him when he was little. For a long time, they just held each other without speaking.

✢ ✢ ✢

The day before the funeral, Wynson answered the door to an Asian woman he had never seen before. He assumed it must be one of his mother's friends come to pay her respects.

"Are you Wynson?" she asked.

He nodded.

"I'm MeiYin."

When this failed to elicit a spark of recognition, she elucidated further. "Your mother's sister."

His aunt? His father must have contacted her. Wynson's parents had almost never talked about her family, and Wynson didn't even know his father knew how to reach them.

"You...you came all the way from Taiwan?" He guided

her to the living room and offered her a drink.

"Yes, I bought a plane ticket as soon as I got your father's letter. It was such a shock after all these years…" She dabbed at her eye. "It's hard to believe she's gone. My *little* sister. First Feng, then Father…"

Feng? Who's Feng? Wynson wondered. He rummaged through his brain for a few moments. "Feng…that's my great-uncle?" he asked tentatively.

"Yes, Feng was Father's mother's brother. He was such fun! We loved when he came over to the house. Always teasing and joking. He was just fifty-two when the stomach cancer took him."

Wynson frowned with a sudden thought. "He had stomach cancer too?"

"Yes. And Father. He died in 2004."

It's genetic?!? The whole of his mother's illness, Wynson had never once stopped to think what her condition might mean to him. Was he carrying a ticking time bomb as well?

His aunt didn't seem to notice his distress. "All these years," she continued, "I wanted to get in touch with SuAnn, especially after Father died, but I didn't know how to reach her or if she would ever forgive me for what I did."

"What you did?" Wynson repeated blankly.

"Didn't they ever tell you?" she asked. "Huh. Well, you know that your mother was secretly engaged to your father, right?"

His aunt wasted no time telling him the story, or to unburden the weight she had carried for all these years. Wynson hadn't exactly known that, but he didn't want to admit his ignorance, so he just nodded.

"Well, the night before the wedding, your mother asked me to be a witness," MeiYin continued. "I had never even met your father. The idea of SuAnn marrying a poor farmer's son and going off to live in America petrified me. I was afraid she would ruin her life.

"So I told our father. I was sure he would put a stop to it. Your grandfather was not a man to be crossed. He immediately confronted SuAnn, forbidding her to marry your father and telling her he would disown her if she did. But she stood her ground. She said she loved your father and she would marry him, even if it meant being poor and losing her family. Father was furious. He left the house and went to find your father.

"I don't know what happened, but I never saw SuAnn again. We were not allowed to speak of her in the house. I always wondered how she was doing, how her life turned out."

Wynson couldn't believe he was just hearing this now. He'd known his mother was estranged from her family, but he'd thought it was because she'd moved to America, not because they disapproved of her marriage. He had a hard time imagining his parents as passionate young lovers risking everything to be together.

"This is a beautiful home," MeiYin said, looking around the large foyer. "Can you tell me, was she happy?" She searched his face for reassurance.

"She was," Wynson promised her. "Very happy."

"Good," she said. "I am glad to hear that. You know, sometimes I envied her, marrying for love. I married a doctor. He was a good man, but..." She shrugged. "Is your father here?"

"I'm afraid not. He had to drop off the musical selections for the service. I'm not sure when he'll be back. Do you want to wait?"

"No, no," she insisted. "I don't want to intrude. I know you have a lot to do. I'll talk to him tomorrow. Just let him know I was here and that I appreciate his letter and… that I'm sorry."

⁘ ⁘ ⁘

The funeral home was filling up. JenJen and her family and MeiYin were up at the front. Some of his parents' friends and his father's business associates Wynson recognized, but many he didn't. LaShawn was there and Jim and Jim's new wife, Gisele, but there was no one Wynson's age.

A couple of his Columbia friends had offered to make the trip, but he'd told them it wasn't necessary. Almost everyone he knew from high school was at an out-of-state college or busy with something as well. The few classmates who were going to school in the area weren't close friends, and he hadn't reached out to let them know. It hadn't seemed worth it at the time, but now he sort of wished he had. Even a casual acquaintance would have been nice.

Suddenly his heart leapt. *Christa!*

His joy was almost instantly tempered when he noticed how Christa was relying on Gabby to guide her into the room. Her head was fixed ahead, not scanning the audience or trying to establish eye contact. Her sight had obviously deteriorated significantly since he'd last seen her.

Wynson jumped out of his seat and rushed down the aisle toward her.

"Hi! Mrs. McMeri." A brief greeting while facing Christa entirely. "Christa!" he said. She did not hear him at first. Then, she swiftly turned toward him, focusing on the sound of his voice.

"Wynson!" There was nothing strained or forced in her smile. It was as if they had never been apart.

"What are you doing here? I thought you were at Arizona State!" he said into the microphone of her CI. "Are you back on break?"

She tilted her head down. "No. I, uh, I'm at home."

"But wh—?"

"It's a long story," she said, cutting him off. "We can talk about it later. I'm so sorry to hear about your mom. I didn't even know she was sick. How are you doing?"

"Oh, I don't know," Wynson admitted. "I think I'm still in shock. It doesn't feel real." Wynson wanted to keep talking to her; he ignored the stares of other guests.

"I can imagine."

The recorded music suddenly cut off as a cue that the service was about to begin.

"Here, let me help you find a seat," offered Wynson, taking her arm. "We'll put you on the outside so Gabby can sit next to you." As he maneuvered her to an empty row, Wynson noticed his father watching them.Not meeting his father's eyes, he got Christa and her mother seated and Gabby situated.

"It means so much to me that you're here. Can we get together later? I'd really like to talk to you."

"Of course. I'd like that. Just text me later."

He hurried back to the front as the funeral director stepped up to the podium. Wynson couldn't seem to focus on what he was saying. His mind kept flitting back to Christa, sitting just a few rows behind him.

Pay attention, he told himself sternly. *This is your mother's* funeral.

Wynson stared at his mother's portrait and had a hard

time recognizing her in the funeral director's remarks. Even though he'd quizzed the family for personal details to make it more individualized, the words felt false coming from someone who had never even known her.

Then it was his father's turn to speak. He was to be the family spokesperson.

JonSun Tang looked out over the crowd.

"I loved SuAnn from the moment I saw her," he began. "It was like lightning struck me. I couldn't believe such a beautiful, smart, high-class woman would stoop down to be with a simple, poor farm boy like me. But she did, and she even gave up everything to come with me to America. She never complained." JonSun started to sob. He choked and lost control.

Wynson walked up, put his arm around his father's shoulder, walked him down, and sat him on an empty seat in the front. He took the paper from his father and walked up to the podium.

He read from the paper—a paper with watermarks, or the marks from teardrops.

"We built a good life together. I worked hard to give SuAnn everything she deserved. And she gave me a wonderful son. We very happy. And then we learned of SuAnn's illness. It wrecked me. I gave up running my business. I wanted to spend every minute we have left with her. Those last months were the hardest I ever had. But they were beautiful too. They reminded me of when we were young, when it was just me and SuAnn. But this time we don't have a life ahead of us; we have a life of memories behind us."

Wynson was shocked to see tears streaming down his father's face.

"I never stopped loving SuAnn, but these last months I

fell in love with her again. And I'll always be glad for that."

Wynson stepped away as the familiar chords of "As Time Goes By" started up. He couldn't begin to count all the times he had heard it throughout his childhood and during his mother's final days.

It was only when the song ended that Wynson realized his own face was wet with tears.

✤ ✤ ✤

The limo ride back from the cemetery was quiet. Both Wynson and his father were caught up in their own thoughts.

"I saw your friend Christa," his father finally said, breaking the silence. Wynson's head shot up. His father seemed to have read his mind. "She is using guide dog now?"

Wynson knew the timing was bad, but he couldn't help himself.

"Dad, I need to talk to you about Christa," he said. "I know why you didn't want me to be with her. You were trying to protect me. I get it. No one wants to see someone they love in pain. You were right. It's hard to see her go through that when I can't do anything about it. But after what you said today in the service, I realized that there is one thing that is even worse than seeing someone you love hurting. And that is not seeing them at all. Dad, didn't you just say that you are *glad* you got to be with Mom when she was sick? That it was a beautiful experience?"

"But that's not the same," his father protested. "We already had life together! We not just starting out."

"Are you saying if you'd known ahead of time that Mom would get sick, you wouldn't have married her?"

"Of course not. But it's not the same."

"I know it isn't *exactly* the same," said Wynson gently. "But it is sort of the same. You know that what Mom had is hereditary, don't you? Did you ever think about that? That maybe *I've* got bad genes too? How would you feel if someone didn't want to marry me because of that?"

His father didn't reply.

"Look," said Wynson, "there's something I want to show you, okay? It'll just take a minute." His father nodded and Wynson asked the limo driver to make a small detour.

"Our old house?" his father asked when he heard the address.

"Yeah. When you see it, maybe you'll understand."

The house was barely out of their way, and soon they had pulled up to the curb. Wynson led his father over to the large wax myrtle in the front yard. There, cut into the trunk, was a heart with the letters "W.T. + C.M." carved inside.

"Wynson Tang loves Christa McMeri," Wynson said. "I did that in the *third grade*. The way you felt about Mom when you first saw her, that's how I felt about Christa. I knew there wasn't ever going to be anyone else for me. Ever. Most people never have a love like that. But we were lucky.

"Dad, I *love* Christa. I want to be with her. I know it isn't going to be easy, but if I can help make her life just the *slightest* bit better by being in it, that's worth it to me. I'm going to do it no matter what, but I'd really like your support."

His father stared at him, his expression unreadable. "If you love her like I love your mother," he finally said, "you must be with her."

"Thanks, Dad," Wynson said. "You don't know how much that means to me."

All I have to do now, Wynson thought as they walked back to the limo, *is convince Christa.*

FLIPPING

✥ ✥ ✥

They decided to meet at a small park near Christa's house. It was somewhere she was comfortable walking to; in fact, she often took Gabby for walks there.

"I'm so sorry about your mom," Christa said. She wore big dark sunglasses. "How are you doing?"

"It's rough, but I'm okay," Wynson said, enunciating clearly so she would be sure to hear him. "It's my dad I'm really worried about. He always looked so strong, but he's falling apart without her."

"His whole world has imploded. It will take him some time to figure out who he is again," Christa said. "It's a hard thing to do. Speaking from personal experience."

"I hope you're not too mad at him for what he said before, about us not being together..."

"It's okay. He wants what he thinks is best for you, just like my parents do. It upset me a lot at the time," Christa admitted, "but now I know that what *really* bothered me was that I believed it myself."

Wynson frowned. "What do you mean?"

"I didn't think I was good enough to be in a relationship."

"But you've always been so confident," Wynson said. "You never let anything or anyone stand in your way. You're like a force of nature!"

"Sure, with *gymnastics*," she said with a smile. "But I realize now that as much as I loved it, I was also using gymnastics as a crutch. It was something safe for me, something I could control. And when I was training seven days a week, I couldn't be expected to have time for anything else, now, could I? It was the perfect excuse for not having friends or a boyfriend..."

"So, are you ready for a boyfriend now?"

"I don't know. I had to do a lot of soul searching when I was disqualified from the Olympic trials and—"

"I heard about that. I'm really sorry. I wish I'd been there."

"It's okay. Really. Actually, it sounds weird to say, but it ended up being the best thing that ever happened to me. Don't get me wrong. I was *devastated* when it happened. But it forced me to figure out who I was if I wasn't a gymnast anymore. My eyesight had started to deteriorate pretty rapidly, so I decided to defer school for a year. I've been living at home, learning Braille and how to get around on my own with Gabby, and basically just getting to know who I am. And you know what? I'm discovering I kind of like me."

"Well, that's no surprise," Wynson said. "I've always liked you." He took her hand and opened her palm up. Slowly, he traced I-heart-U. "That hasn't changed, Christa. My mother's death made me realize what's really important in life. It's the people we love. I'm not naïve. I know that we're going to have a lot of challenges ahead. But nobody's perfect and nobody knows what the future holds. The one thing I *do* know is I missed out on being with you this past year. I wish I had been there for you through everything you went through. That's a mistake I don't ever want to repeat. So, what do you say, why don't we be imperfect together?"

"Wynson," she finally said, "we may not be perfect, but I think we just might be perfect for each other."

And Wynson looked at Christa with her strong, square shoulders and jaw and her piercing, brilliant blue eyes that couldn't see well but saw him better than anyone… and he knew she was telling the truth.

FLIPPING

❖ ❖ ❖

Wynson contacted Columbia to let them know he would be taking an indefinite leave of absence. He told his father it was just a break, but he knew in his heart that he wouldn't be going back. His father wasn't happy about his decision, but he didn't have the energy to fight. And, although his father didn't say so, Wynson could tell his presence was a comfort. The enormous dream home was empty without SuAnn, and his father needed a tether to life while he got back on his feet.

Wynson developed an early-morning ritual. He would wake up at sunrise, slip on his flip-flops, and quietly retreat to the shoreline. He walked along the beach and felt his mother in the wind as it ruffled his ebony hair. Sometimes he walked slowly and reflectively, absorbing the sun's warmth and gaining inspiration for the day.

Other times he would break into a jog barefooted. The seagulls would scurry away and caw at him as he ran through their midst. Something about the sting in his lungs and the ache in his calves from running on the unsteady sand revitalized him. *Now I know why Christa works out so hard*, he thought. His heart felt like it was exploding and blood surged through his veins.

Those moments gave him clarity. He recalled his words to Christa from weeks before: "Life is like a series of obstacle courses—perform well on tests, make straight As, build a college résumé, get into school, get a job."

Now, Wynson wanted to get off the treadmill and learn who *he* was. He realized Christa's wholehearted pursuit of her gymnastics dream was a huge reason he loved and felt inspired by her. He wanted to shoot for dreams so huge it surprised him, but he also wanted it to be authentic.

FLIPPING

The only thing he was sure of was his love for Christa. She had been the driving passion in his life. But she was a person, not a project. He needed a vocation, and he didn't think the law was it. He could handle the academic work, but he didn't have a passion for the law, and the adversarial process cut against his core. He hated confrontation, and preferred collaboration to competition.

Looking back over his life, he realized the times he felt the most useful and productive were when he was helping someone. Caring for his mother, helping Christa adjust to her blindness, even now, supporting his father through the grieving process. Maybe he'd go into social work or therapy. Or medicine. For some reason, his father had always seemed to steer him away from being a medical doctor. Strange, he thought, since most Asian parents wanted nothing more than a physician son.

He didn't feel a rush to make a decision. For the first time in his life, he was content to just be. He got a job as a park ranger, cooked meals for his father, worked in the garden, and spent time with Christa. He didn't know what the future held. But it didn't matter. Because they'd be facing it together.

Acknowledgments

Although the plot and the characters in the manuscript are fictional, this book could not have materialized without the people whom I have encountered and received assistance from in my life.

I would like to express my appreciation to Dr. Bill Takeshita, Chief of Optometry, and the entire staff at the Center for the Partially Sighted in Los Angeles for their services and education for low-vision patients. Your seminars are insightful for professionals and patients.

I am indebted to the House Ear Clinic, especially to the late Dr. William House. Your support to the mother of a deaf child inspired me to develop one of the main characters, Christa, and her family.

I am particularly grateful for the assistance given by Tanya Berenson, Will Ezzard, and Yefim Furman at the Los Angeles School of Gymnastics. Thank you for taking your precious time to answer my numerous gymnastics-related questions.

I wish to acknowledge the various Usher syndrome organizations for their devotion to patients throughout the progress of this disease and for their endeavor to fund research for the treatment of this genetic disorder.

I also appreciate all of the people who shared their fear, anguish, and confusion when blindness was bestowed upon them and showed me their courage in coping with the loss of their eyesight.

Last but not the least, I wish to express my heartfelt gratitude to everyone who provided support, encouragement, and criticism through the writing, editing, and publishing of this book. I am especially grateful for the assistance given by Adrienne Miller, who diligently coordinated all parties through the production.

Appendix 1

Gymnastics

Amânar or Shewfelt: An artistic gymnastics vault named after the first gymnast to perform it at a World Championship or Olympic Game: Simona Amânar at the 2000 Olympics for women, and Kyle Shewfelt at the 2000 Olympics for men. The vault contains two and a half twists in the backward salto.

Arabian Double Front: An Arabian front (a half twist into front somersault) done with two front somersaults instead of just one. It can be done in any of the tumbling positions, either tuck, pike, open, or even in layout. It is currently a popular pass in international elite artistic gymnastics, for both men and women. It is highly rated in difficulty and meets the requirement for front tumbling without resorting to front combination tumbling passes.

Back Walkover: An acrobatic maneuver in which a person transitions from a standing position to a gymnastic back bridge and then back to a standing position again, undergoing one complete rotation of the body in the process.

Balance Beam: The gymnast completes a choreographed routine with a mount, leaps, jumps, flips, turns, and a dismount on a padded wooden beam approximately four feet high and four inches wide. The exercise may not be longer than ninety seconds.

Cartwheel: A sideways rotary movement of the body, performed by bringing the hands to the floor one at a time while the body inverts. When both hands are on the floor, the legs travel over the body and feet return to the floor one at a time, ending with the performer standing upright.

Code of Points: The rulebook for gymnastics. The code of points specifies the difficulty value of all skills, as well as outlines requirements that must be fulfilled for each event.

Compulsory: A routine in which the elements are predetermined by an organization such as USAG or FIG. All gymnasts competing with compulsory routines must perform specified skills in a specified order. Compulsory routines have been eliminated from higher level gymnastics competitions to allow for more time to develop optional routines.

Dismount: A method by which the gymnast leaves a piece of apparatus at the end of a performance or an exercise.

Elite artistic gymnasts: Elite artistic gymnasts are the best gymnasts in the world, competing for rankings and medals. Elite gymnastics begin once a gymnast has surpassed level 10 and meets the elite requirements. In the United States, elite gymnasts are members of USA Gymnastics and follow the Federation de Internationale Code of Points.

Events: The four women's events in gymnastics are floor, uneven bars, beam, vault. The six men's events are floor, pommel horse, rings, vault, parallel bars, high bar.

Fabrichnova Double Twisting Double Back: To perform a double twisting double back dismount, a gymnast must swing forward, release the high bar, and flip backward 720 degrees while also twisting 720 degrees on her axis—and then landing on her feet. When done in the tucked position—that is, with bent knees—this skill is called the Fabrichnova, named after Soviet great gymnast Oksana Fabrichnova.

Flip: Rotation about the transverse, or the horizontal axis. This axis runs left to right. When you are doing a forward roll, you are rotating about the transverse axis.

Floor Exercise: The gymnast performs a choreographed routine to music of her choice. The routine usually consists of four or five tumbling passes, as well as leaps, jumps, and dance moves, and cannot be longer than ninety seconds. The floor mat is forty feet by forty feet and is usually made of carpeting over padded foam and springs.

Handspring: An acrobatic move in which a person executes a complete revolution of the body by lunging headfirst from an upright position into a vertical position and then pushing off (i.e., "springing") from the floor with the hands so as to leap back to an upright position.

Handstand: The act of supporting the body in a stable, inverted vertical position by balancing on the hands.

Levels in Gymnastics: In the United States, USA Gymnastics (USAG) is the governing body that runs the prevalent competitive system. This system is called the Junior Olympic, or JO, system. The ultimate goal of JO is to create elite-level athletes. In order to reach the upper echelon of JO, gymnasts must pass through ten levels.

Optional: A routine in which the gymnast may perform skills of their choosing under the constraints of special requirements. The skills can be performed in any order but must fit the requirements as specified in the FIG code of points.

Routine: A routine is a sequence of skills in an event. The number and difficulty of skills depend on the competition format and skill level of the competitors Salto: Another term for flip or roll. A rotation about the transverse axis.

Split (commonly referred to as splits or the splits): A physical position in which the legs are in line with each other and extended in opposite directions.

Twist: A rotation about the longitudinal, or vertical, axis. This is the axis that runs from your head to your feet. When you spin in a circle while standing, you are "twisting." A right twist is defined as the right shoulder going backward, the converse for a left twist.

Uneven Bars: The gymnast performs swings, release moves, pirouettes, and a dismount using two horizontal bars set at different heights. The lower bar is usually about five feet off the ground, and the high bar is about eight feet from the floor.

Vault: The gymnast runs down a runway, jumps onto a springboard, and is propelled over a vaulting "table" about four feet off the ground.

Appendix 2

Usher Syndrome and Hearing Impairment

American Sign Language (ASL): is the predominant sign language of deaf communities in the United States and most of Anglophone Canada.

Auditory Brainstem Response (ABR): gives information about the inner ear (cochlea) and brain pathways for hearing. This test is also sometimes referred to as auditory evoked potential (AEP). The test can be used with children or others who have a difficult time with conventional behavioral methods of hearing screening. The ABR is also indicated for a person with signs, symptoms, or complaints suggesting a type of hearing loss in the brain or a brain pathway. The ABR is performed by pasting electrodes on the head—similar to electrodes placed around the heart when an electrocardiogram is run—and recording brain wave activity in response to sound. The person being tested rests quietly or sleeps while the test is performed. No response is necessary. ABR can also be used as a screening test in newborn hearing screening programs. When used as a screening test, only one intensity or loudness level is checked, and the baby either passes or fails the screen.

Audiogram: is a graph showing the results of the pure-tone hearing tests. It illustrates the type, degree, and configuration of hearing loss. The frequency or pitch of the sound is referred to in hertz (Hz). The intensity or loudness of the sound is measured in decibels (dB). The responses are recorded on a chart called an audiogram that shows intensity levels for each frequency tested.

The Center for the Partially Sighted: is an American nonprofit organization with the goal of promoting independent living for people with visual impairments. The center was founded in 1978 by Sam Genensky and two associates as an outreach program of the Santa Monica Hospital (now the Santa Monica – UCLA Medical Center). The Center works with persons who have partial to profound vision loss as a result of macular degeneration, glaucoma, strokes, cataracts, complications of diabetes, retinitis pigmentosa, cortical visual impairment, retinopathy of prematurity, atrophy of the optic nerve, albinism, and eye injury. It provides several services to persons with these conditions, including optometric counseling, life counseling, rehabilitation assistance, and specialized programs such as residential visits to advise in making living areas more livable. (https://en.wikipedia.org/wiki/)

Cochlear implant (CI): is a surgically implanted electronic device that provides a sense of sound to a person who is profoundly deaf or severely hard of hearing. A cochlear implant isn't a hearing aid, which makes sounds louder. A cochlear implant is a small device that is placed in your inner ear through surgery. It works by sending impulses directly to your auditory nerve, which carries signals to your brain.

Deaf culture: is the set of social beliefs, behaviors, art, literary traditions, history, values, and shared institutions of communities that are influenced by deafness and use sign languages as the main means of communication.

The House Ear Institute (HEI): is a nonprofit 501(c)(3) organization, based in Los Angeles, California, and dedicated to advancing hearing science through research, education, and global hearing health to improve quality of life. Established in 1946 by Howard P. House, M.D., as the Los Angeles Foundation of Otology, and later renamed for its founder, the House Ear Institute has been engaged in the scientific exploration of the auditory system from the ear canal to the cortex of the brain for over sixty-nine years. (https://en.wikipedia.org/wiki/House_Ear_Institute)

John Tracy Clinic: is a private, nonprofit education center for infants and preschool children with hearing loss in Los Angeles, California. It was founded by Louise Treadwell Tracy, wife of actor Spencer Tracy, in 1942. It provides free, parent-centered services worldwide. The Clinic has over sixty years of expertise in the spoken language option, called oralism. The Clinic offers worldwide family services, local family services, professional education, preschool, hearing testing, and more.
(https://en.wikipedia.org/wiki/John_Tracy_Clinic)

Mapping a Cochlear Implant: Mapping (or MAPping) is the term for programming a cochlear implant to the specifications and needs of its user. MAPs are programs that help to optimize the cochlear implant user's access to sound by adjusting the input to the electrodes on the array that is implanted into the cochlea. The cochlear implant processor is connected to the audiologist's computer for MAPping. Using a series of "beeps," and measuring the CI user's response, the audiologist sets T and C-levels for each electrode. T-levels, or thresholds, are the softest sounds the CI users can detect. C-levels (also sometimes called M-Levels), are comfortable loudness levels that are tolerable for the CI user. The audiologist might also adjust the stimulation rate or programming strategy used for the MAP—these refer to the various computer algorithms and programs used to translate acoustic sound (what people with typical hearing perceive) into the correct combination of electrode stimulations to give the cochlear implant user that same sensation of sound. (http://cochlearimplantonline.com/site/mapping-a-cochlearimplant/)

Hearing Screening Tests: Hearing screening programs are called "universal" newborn because they are set up to test all babies. All babies can and should have their hearing tested before they leave the hospital, or within three weeks of leaving the hospital. If a baby is born at home, a hearing test should be completed before he or she is two months old. When a baby fails the screening tests, he or she is referred for more detailed, diagnostic hearing testing. If a hearing loss is found, then hearing aids and therapy services are started to help the baby learn to listen and speak.

Oral/aural: an approach to deaf education that emphasizes auditory training, articulation ability, and lip-reading. One of the primary communication methods used in education of deaf children.

Retinitis pigmentosa (RP): is a group of genetic disorders that affect the retina's ability to respond to light. This inherited disease causes a slow loss of vision, beginning with decreased night vision and loss of peripheral (side) vision.

Eventually, blindness results. Unfortunately, there is no cure for RP.
(http://www.geteyesmart.org/eyesmart/diseases/retinitis-pigmentosa.cfm)

Sensorineural hearing loss (SNHL): occurs when there is damage to the inner ear (cochlea), or to the nerve pathways from the inner ear to the brain. Most of the time, SNHL cannot be medically or surgically corrected. This is the most common type of permanent hearing loss. SNHL reduces the ability to hear faint sounds. Even when speech is loud enough to hear, it may still be unclear or the sound muffled. (http://www.asha.org/public/hearing/Sensorineural-Hearing-Loss)

Signing Exact English (SEE-II, sometimes Signed Exact English): is a system of manual communication that strives to be an exact representation of English vocabulary and grammar. It is one of a number of such systems in use in English-speaking countries.

Speech Banana: The speech banana is a term used to describe the area where the phonemes, or sounds of human speech, appear on an audiogram. When the phonemes are plotted out on the audiogram, they take the shape of a banana; therefore, audiologists and other speech professionals refer to that area as the speech banana. While many other sounds fall outside of the speech banana, audiologists are most concerned with the frequencies within the speech banana because a hearing loss in those frequencies can affect a child's ability to learn language. (http://www.agbell.org/SpeechBanana/)

Total Communication (TC): is an approach to Deaf education that aims to make use of a number of modes of communication such as signed, oral, auditory, written, and visual aids, depending on the particular needs and abilities of the child.

Usher syndrome: is the most common condition that affects both hearing and vision. A syndrome is a disease or disorder that has more than one feature or symptom. The major symptoms of Usher syndrome are hearing loss and an eye disorder called retinitis pigmentosa, or RP. RP causes nightblindness and a loss of peripheral vision (side vision) through the progressive degeneration of the retina. The retina is a light-sensitive tissue at the back of the eye and is crucial for vision. As RP progresses, the field of vision narrows—a condition known as "tunnel vision"—until only central vision (the ability to see straight ahead) remains.
http://www.nidcd.nih.gov/health/hearing/pages/usher.aspx

About the Author

Dr. Eichin Chang-Lim was born in Taiwan. She earned her doctorate in optometry from Southern California College of Optometry and is currently in a private practice with her husband near L.A. They have one son, Theodore, and one daughter, Victoria, and live in Orange County.

Eichin is passionate about writing, acting, and enjoys listening to classical music and opera.

Learn more about Eichin Chang-Lim:

www.eichinchanglim.com

Made in the USA
Lexington, KY
24 November 2018